TERROR LOVE

Married to Gilbert Brand, Kathryn imagines her marriage to be a happy one. It's studded with the parties of her husband's rich, socialite friends. But their attendance at a party given by his business associate, Victor Milo, tarnishes Brand's suave image. Kathryn discovers Brand attempting to strangle another guest, the nightclub singer Claudia, who becomes Kathryn's bitterest enemy. Then her world begins to crumble as she learns that Brand is an unscrupulous criminal . . . and she begins a descent into terror.

NORMAN LAZENBY

TERROR LOVE

Complete and Unabridged

LINFORD
Leicester

First published in Great Britain

First Linford Edition
published 2012

British Library CIP Data

Lazenby, Norman A. (Norman Austin)
   Terror love. - - (Linford mystery library)
   1. Suspense fiction.
   2. Large type books.
   I. Title II. Series
   813.5′4–dc23

   ISBN 978–1–4448–1185–8

Published by
F. A. Thorpe (Publishing)
Anstey, Leicestershire

Set by Words & Graphics Ltd.
Anstey, Leicestershire
Printed and bound in Great Britain by
T. J. International Ltd., Padstow, Cornwall

This book is printed on acid-free paper

1

TERROR LOVE

1

Strangler!

My life with Gilbert Brand had been exciting — a day-to-day whirlwind of dining out, theatre-going, seeing people, travelling. But at twenty-one years of age, though outwardly sophisticated, I was deep inside of me still a girl who had left school only three years ago.

Three years! And married to Gilbert for the last twelve months! My placid schooldays now seemed like an existence that had never really belonged to me.

I had no parents, only a somewhat decrepit guardian of eighty who lived in the Midlands and to whom I was some vague responsibility to be pacified by an occasional remittance and a letter asking about my health! The money was always welcome, for Gilbert and I lived extravagantly; the letter was read with amusement and quickly forgotten.

But there were times when stark, frightening facts peeped out at me through this hectic, superficial life. Where did Gilbert obtain all the money he spent so recklessly? Why did he always tease me when I asked about his work, seeking to be his helpmate and not a pretty, gay ornament? Where did he go when he went away on his frequent missions without me?

I remember the day I inquired too deeply into these matters.

He was making love to me, holding my face to his with his soft hands.

'But, darling, why should you worry about money?' he teased.

Oh, he loved me. I knew he loved me!

'Everyone has to worry about money,' I laughed. 'It has to be earned, before it can be spent.'

His eyes were blue, and sometimes, in certain strong lights, the blueness was startling. We were strongly contrasting types. He was dark, and very tall, but though I, too, was tall, my hair was fair. But our love was a thrilling, intimate possession.

'Silly girl — or should I say, lovely grey eyes?' He kissed me again. 'For goodness sake never mention money to me. I have my income. There are many easy ways of earning more money — simple ways of doubling one's capital. Only a fool works like a slave for someone else.'

There it was again! In the last few months, time and time again, Gilbert had disturbed me with such ideas. I never attempted to argue with him. But somewhere in my heart I longed to cry, 'Gilbert — my Gilbert, it is not true! One should be proud to work, proud of one's abilities!'

I was so delightfully in love that I was determined nothing should spoil it. We would go on forever, eager for each other. Living a modern life of gaiety and thrills.

It was evening. We were having cocktails in our flat before leaving to dine at the Superb. We had started to talk about the rent of the flat — at least, looking back, I realise I had started the subject. Twice he had evaded my gentle questions, quickly turning our conversation to another topic.

And then he had leaned towards me, cupped my face with his hands, kissed me.

After a while, he said: 'To set your mind at rest, my dear Kathryn, I'll write the cheque out now.'

It was on the tip of my tongue to say that four weeks were due. But Gilbert knew as well as I how much he owed the agents, and I was silent as I watched him write his cheque for sixty pounds.

We were living in a beautifully furnished flat in Chelsea.

Everything was exquisite. Luxurious carpets covered every inch of the four rooms, and the bathroom was a dream from Hollywood. The drawing room had been decorated by a well-known artist, beautiful Chinese vases abounded, and every day I bought flowers.

Gilbert went to his bureau, slipped the cheque into an envelope and addressed it, then pushed the envelope into an inside pocket of his evening suit.

'There you are, my dear.' He smiled. 'It shall be posted and your worries ended. But why you should even bother to think about such rotten affairs, I can't imagine.'

He teased me a lot, I knew, but I loved him.

I jumped up. The skirt of my emerald dress fell in sweeping lines to the floor.

'Isn't the taxi late?' I asked. 'I'm simply dying to see Claudia at the Superb.'

I was young, impulsive. Gilbert always said my eyes glowed when I was excited. But I seldom thought about myself.

Claudia was a singer. Somehow Gilbert knew her and introduced her to me. Claudia was the new sensation at the Superb.

But the taxi driver came to the flat on time, as Gilbert had ordered, and when we entered the Superb we were shown to our favourite table. The nightclub, extremely modern and exclusive, was decorated in the most bizarre style. We were well-known, and a smiling, bowing waiter showed us to our table, where Gilbert at once ordered dinner.

Later we danced, gliding along to the strains of a waltz in slow time. The diminutive floor was not too crowded and Gilbert and I attracted some notice, I know. The band played softly the latest tune — the absurd, lilting 'Lovely You'. Oh, it was delightful!

Little did I know that this was my last carefree dance with Gilbert Brand, that fate was to take the little bubble of our existence and whirl it crazily to destruction! As for Gilbert — but that was the bitter future! I was to encounter police, stark fear, and Hugh! Yes, dear Hugh!

But now we were dancing at the Superb and my life was perfect. I could not sincerely understand how unhappiness existed. I had never been unhappy.

Too late I realized how superficial my life with Gilbert really was.

A little later, after we had returned to our table, Claudia came to an upraised dais to sing. A spotlight was played upon her statuesque body wreathed in silk, and the restaurant lights were dimmed. Claudia was new. Her husky voice could sway the whole audience to spontaneous applause.

Her song over, she came towards us, out of the whole crowded restaurant, and Gilbert smilingly helped her with her chair.

'Kathryn, how gorgeous you look!' Claudia had a drawling low-toned voice. 'Honestly, pet, I'm quite envious of your dress.'

There was little about me Claudia should have envied for she was amazingly attractive in her own right. Her auburn hair was not, perhaps, natural, but it was definitely striking and she wore it in a long pageboy style.

Of course, I knew the truth about Claudia. Her accent was cultivated, even somewhat theatrical. I had to admit she was more than sophisticated; men crowded round her and not always the right type of men. But she loved it. Gilbert had told me about her long struggle for some sort of recognition on the stage and cabaret: how she had risen from the bottom rung of third-rate stage shows. She was hard. I knew that and admired her while I felt inwardly shocked at some aspects of her life. She was about twenty-eight, and had known more men than was good for her.

I never felt jealous when Gilbert laughed and talked with other women. I was so absolutely sure of our love that such emotions did not exist.

'Would you like to go to a party tonight, Gilbert?' Claudia asked, then looked at me.

Gilbert's blue eyes were never round like a child's. Even when they were grave or humorous they had a fascinating narrow way of looking at you as if he was a man who restrained his impulses.

'Would you like it, Kathryn?' he asked gently.

And I knew that if I demurred he would courteously decline the invitation. But, of course, I never turned down the chance of a party.

'Always ready for a party!' I returned saucily.

Claudia — her real name was Jean Metcalfe — retorted:

'Well, party time is after the show. Don't be too tight. There will be plenty to drink later.'

'Who is the kind person throwing the party?' Gilbert inquired lazily.

It seldom mattered whom the host might be.

'Victor Milo,' said Claudia slowly.

'Oh, is it?' He picked up his glass deliberately.

But when I glanced at him, his smile had vanished. He began a yawn — and stifled it.

'Perhaps it would be better if we toddled home.' Then he added, 'Too many late nights, you know.'

'I think Milo would be particularly gratified to see you,' said Claudia calmly.

A threat? At that precise moment I should have laughed the idea to scorn, but now I know the truth.

'Well,' he paused, 'why not?' He smiled, and raised his glass.

We left by taxi for Victor Milo's large Bayswater flat. I had never met the man and, curious, I asked Gilbert about him.

'He is not English,' said Gilbert. 'He is an American of Italian extraction, I believe. He's a giant of a man. Lives too well, I should imagine. He's very wealthy.'

'I have never heard you talk about him,' I said.

There was surprise in his retort. 'Haven't I?'

At Milo's flat the scene was typical of

many parties we had attended. Laughing, drinking couples lounged everywhere. Conversation was continuous and punctuated by shrieks of laughter from some showgirls. A manservant made constant journeys to a mysterious kitchen, bringing fresh glasses and sandwiches. A young man with a drooping cigarette tapped expertly at a baby-grand piano. When Claudia, Gilbert and I walked in we were at once greeted by several acquaintances.

'Hello, my pets!' This from the terribly lean actress, Margery Sands, who has been divorced more times than I can remember.

'It's the Brands!' exclaimed other voices, and people came crowding around.

Soon we were sorted out, and I was introduced to our host. Victor Milo. He smiled at me from a large, white, flabby face. He was positively mountainous. His evening suit was faultless, and unlike most bulky men he wore it perfectly. He had rings on the first finger of each hand; I have always disliked men who sported rings.

'I'm certainly pleased to meet you,

Mrs. Brand,' said Milo, in a throaty American intonation.

'Kathryn,' I corrected with a gay laugh.

'Gilbert is a shrewder boy than I suspected,' he commented, watching me closely.

I was not too hazy with champagne to wonder at this remark. Was Gilbert shrewd? After half-an-hour of gaiety round the piano, I looked about for my husband. I had thought he was somewhere behind me. I had been singing with the young man at the piano, surrounded by a large group. I whirled round, flushed with excitement. He was not a very melodious pianist, but no one cared.

I eased myself from the crush. I looked round the room. Gilbert was certainly not to be seen.

I walked to a passage that led to a dressing room, where I had been told I could make up. It was an ornate room, which gave on to a bedroom. How many rooms there were in Victor Milo's flat, I could not tell. It seemed very large and luxurious, though I preferred the modest good taste of our Chelsea home.

The dressing room was very disordered. I stared round, looked at myself critically in a large dressing mirror.

And then a horrible scene met my eyes! The long mirror was reflecting two people like a screen. At first I laughed harshly, thinking I must be drunk and seeing things. Then I wheeled.

Two people were standing inside the bedroom opposite the dressing room door. The man was Gilbert and his hands were round the throat of a girl. I beat down the scream that rose in my throat. I ran to the bedroom, tugged madly at Gilbert, exerting all my strength to tear away his killing hands from the girl.

I had found my husband in a murderous rage nearly strangling Claudia!

2

The Private Investigator

He turned as I intervened, shock draining away the rage in his face.

'Gilbert! Gilbert! What do you think you are doing?' I cried.

He released Claudia. I saw the livid marks on her white neck. Though Gilbert's rage had sunk out of sight like a stone in water, Claudia's fury was still mounting. Her stark fear had vanished with my intervention, and now her anger blazed forth.

'Your precious husband is trying to murder me,' she spat.

Gilbert gripped my arm. 'Get out of here, Kathryn! I'll explain later!'

'You can explain now!' sneered Claudia. She touched the red marks on her painful neck. Beneath her flame-coloured dress her breasts heaved.

Gilbert swung again. He was dangerously calm.

'I lost my head, and I apologise, Claudia. Kathryn, please go. I must talk to Claudia.'

'Why can't I stay?' I asked quietly.

With an effort he controlled his exasperation.

'This is a matter which concerns only Claudia and myself.'

'Surely I'm entitled to more explanation than that?'

His blue eyes gleamed in an ominous way.

'Very well. I shall explain later.'

I trembled, but continued firmly.

'I'd prefer to hear it now.' Then I choked a little. 'Oh, darling, please explain to me!'

Suddenly he smiled. As he smiled, I relaxed, too, and waited for his next words more calmly.

'Poor Kathryn, you've caught Claudia and me in a nasty argument. I admit I lost my temper. We — we — started to argue about Victor Milo. I said I disliked him, and Claudia became simply furious. She contradicted me — and I — I — lost my head in a crazy manner. I wish you had not come along.'

Relief flooded me as I looked into his

quizzical blue eyes. I forgot he might have killed Claudia in his mad rage. I longed for an adequate explanation. Eagerly I accepted what to anyone else must have seemed a curiously lame story.

I even ignored Claudia's contemptuous expression.

'Please come home, Gilbert,' I begged. 'You're tired. Your nerves are all on edge.'

'His nerves,' said Claudia coolly, 'are okay.' She was calmer now. 'If he treats you like this, my pet, I pity you, but perhaps you like being manhandled.'

And then I think I realised how much Claudia hated me. I ignored the taunt, pressed Gilbert's arm. He went with me — slowly. In the passage, he muttered: 'I'll get my coat. We'll find Victor Milo and say good night.'

I got my cloak, too, and we got away with a minimum of farewells. Soon we were in the street. A few yards from the block of flats that housed Milo's place, Gilbert stopped to light a cigarette for me and himself. He flicked at a tiny gold lighter.

The flame spurted, and as we paused the street seemed very quiet. Two hundred yards down the street, the Bayswater Road ran at right angles and we thought we would find a taxi there.

Suddenly a voice said, 'Pardon me, would you give me a light? Got no matches, and my lighter just won't work.'

The man who approached us so silently seemed to have stepped from some doorway.

Gilbert was curt. He held out his lighter without answering.

The stranger was as tall as Gilbert, and in the subdued street lighting his face seemed rugged and brooding. I have always been observant. I thought I saw a man who would smile slowly and infrequently. He was about thirty. His hat was American in type, and the broad brim suited him. He was wearing an expensive raglan coat. One hand was in his pocket but the other was ungloved, and I saw it was fine-fingered. He held a cigarette to his mouth.

He blew out smoke and said, 'Victor Milo throws expensive parties.'

'Are you a friend of Milo?'

'No. Is Claudia at the party?'

'Look here, what the devil has it to do with you?' snapped Gilbert.

'My name is Hugh Maxwell. We'll be seeing each other a lot, perhaps.'

Gilbert laughed curtly. 'Indeed, I hardly think so.'

The other man looked up at the lighted windows of Victor Milo's flat. A street light threw a wan ray upon his profile. I thought he was handsome in a rugged, masculine way. Certainly he had not Gilbert's regular cast of features.

'Jason Selby would be gratified to learn that Milo throws parties while his victims worry themselves to their graves,' said Hugh Maxwell suddenly.

'I don't know what you mean.'

'Oh, you do, Brand. You do.'

And the other put his cigarette back between his lips, and then he looked steadily at me.

I had been scrutinising him curiously, wondering at the strange turn in the conversation. When he stared at me, I returned his gaze coolly. At the moment his grey eyes were sombre, but I had a peculiar feeling that those eyes could light up with real understanding.

'Selby is pretty bad,' said Hugh Maxwell. 'His investments are not so good as they once seemed. He has lost money — in more ways than one. Tell Victor Milo to lay off.'

Gilbert applied an impelling pressure to my arm. I moved a step.

'If you want to talk to me alone,' said the other man quietly, 'I have an office in Holborn. You'll find me at 7, Carter Street. I'm a private investigator. When you get home, you can phone Victor Milo and tell him Selby has hired me. Milo won't lose any sleep, and Selby is in a bad way. I think Milo should know that — if he can remember Selby among the other victims.'

For the second time that night my heart beat with frantic, fearful rapidity. Who was this detective? Why should he pick on Gilbert?

And then, taking my arm, my husband strode off, suppressed anger in his whole attitude.

I was afraid to ask questions, though many trembled on my lips. What on earth did Hugh Maxwell mean by Victor Milo's victims? Who was Jason Selby? Why should Milo be interested in him, and how did Gilbert fit in with all this? Was Hugh Maxwell mad?

Looking back I know that evening was the beginning of my torturing doubts about Gilbert.

We found a taxi and went home. I went straight to our bedroom, changed into a comfortable wrap of blue silk, which had been one of Gilbert's frequent presents. The door was open, and suddenly I heard the muffled tones of Gilbert's voice. He was in the drawing room, at the telephone. For a moment I stood irresolute, then I reached for the bedside receiver, which I knew was on an extension line.

Gilbert was speaking.

'I tell you, Milo, Selby is dangerous. He can't know what he is doing, but he's dangerous. This private dick didn't beat about the bush. He asked about Claudia, too. He's trying to pin something on somebody.'

'Don't worry,' came Victor Milo's throaty reply. 'A private detective in this country is a nobody. Selby knows better than to contact the police. What good will this do him? If he squawks to the police — through his 'tec — he'll be ruined. I'll sure attend to that.'

'There must be something,' insisted Gilbert.

'Let Selby hire as many 'tecs as he likes. He daren't authorise one of them to approach the police. I've got Selby, and he knows it. The old fool! But you can call on Mr. Maxwell tomorrow and tell him that if he becomes unpleasant there is an organisation in London which will rub him out.'

'Thanks for the job — calls for my usual polished touch!' sneered Gilbert. 'I could do with some more money, Milo.'

'I gave you five hundred not so long ago.'

'I know, but it's gone. Living is horribly expensive.'

'And you're the most expensive man I've hired — but I'll keep you on,' rapped the other's voice. 'See me tomorrow at 10 a.m. I might assign you to get Selby to close his account for a cash sum, but I don't know.'

'And what about my money?'

'You'll get something.'

It seemed to be the end of the conversation, and I hurriedly replaced the phone. I went over to the bed and lay down quickly. If Gilbert entered the room, I would pretend to be half-asleep.

But the moment I closed my eyes, my head reeled. All the events of the evening acquired a new, horrible significance, topped by a telephone conversation about which there could be no doubt!

Gilbert was a crook, working for Victor Milo who was also apparently a modern, big-time criminal! They had talked coolly of 'rubbing-out' Hugh Maxwell! And surely Milo was blackmailing the man called Selby?

So this was Gilbert's way of earning money to support us in our whirlwind London life! This was his preference, his contemptuous answer to my light-hearted talk of work!

I lay on the silk coverlet with my hands clenched. My eyes were forced open — ghastly, inescapable fears came into my mind to torture me. I stared at the ceiling. I was dry-eyed and fearful.

'Gilbert! Oh, Gilbert!' I whispered.

For a moment I had a mad impulse to rush out to him, beg him to throw over his connection with Victor Milo. But I was held back by a new and dreadful thought. For the first time in my life I saw the key to Gilbert's nature in this revelation. Gilbert would not be turned from his dreams of easy money by me or anyone else. This life he had chosen was typical of Gilbert Brand. Nothing else would suit him. Somehow I had always known he had a hard streak but I had been proud of it. After all, he was a *man*. I, his wife, was only a girl, and I had been secretly thrilled at a man's firmness.

No it would he disastrous to rush to him pleading for him to reform. He would turn from me in contempt. He would mock me. I would have to pretend to suspect nothing while I planned desperately for some way out.

Gilbert's conversation with Victor Milo had not told me much about their crooked activities. I wondered about Hugh Maxwell's references to other victims. I remembered every word the private investigator had uttered. He had said there were victims worrying themselves to their graves while Milo held parties.

A startling idea then occurred to me. Why not visit Hugh Maxwell tomorrow and ask him frank questions about Milo and my husband?

I told myself fiercely that I would do everything in my power to help Gilbert. Perhaps there was a way in which he could be torn from a crooked life.

Gilbert entered the bedroom as I lay on the bed. I had seen him approach, and I closed my eyes. He came and, as he thought, wakened me with a kiss.

'Tired, darling?'

I smiled faintly.

'A little.'

Not a word about Claudia or Hugh Maxwell. Certainly no remark about talking to Victor Milo on the phone. I wondered what he would say if I asked him whom he had been talking to. On an impulse, I said drowsily: 'Been phoning, darling?'

His eyes narrowed.

I said ingenuously: 'I thought I heard your voice, Gilbert.'

'As a matter of fact, I have been phoning. I've left my confounded hat at Milo's.'

And it was true. He had left his hat in the whirl of our farewells. It was not surprising, for he was accustomed to going out without a hat at times.

'You can buy another,' I said lazily.

He nodded. Then he turned and his eyes were strange.

'You love me, don't you, my sweet?'

I flung my arms round his neck and strained him to me passionately. 'I do! I do!'

'That's all I want to know.'

Oh, the heaven of being kissed by Gilbert! I forgot the whole horrible sequence of events which had planted my mind with suspicions. I kissed him hungrily. He pressed his mouth to mine.

And then the phone bell rang in the other room. Gilbert raised his head.

'Let it ring,' he said with a grin.

But there was shrill insistence in the trilling bell. He reluctantly rose and strolled out of the room.

I did not grab the extension. With Gilbert's warm kisses still on my lips, I waited in uncertainty.

He came back.

'Believe it or not,' he said, with an easy laugh, 'but I've got to go along to Milo's. It's not about my hat either. It seems there's a bloke with Milo who wants to talk investments. They're still going strong down there. I think I'll run down, if it's all the same to you, Kathryn. Might be something in it for me.'

I could not resist the retort: 'I thought you said you disliked Victor Milo!'

He said curtly: 'I do, but business is different.'

He dressed, put on his overcoat and found another hat. He kissed me and then was gone.

The minutes seemed ages as I lay thinking furiously. Then the phone rang again. I picked up the instrument.

'Hello,' I said. 'Mrs. — '

'Follow your husband,' said a voice abruptly. 'You might save him from death! Hurry!'

3

Kidnapped

The brief warning was snapped out so rapidly that I stood in amazement, holding the phone. Then, realizing the line was dead, I replaced the receiver and dashed madly into the bedroom.

I dressed in wild haste, donning an old tweed costume and throwing a coat loosely about my shoulders. I did not bother about stockings or a hat. Within sixty seconds of the warning — or was it a threat? — I was in the car park, hurrying towards the road which ran past the block of flats.

And then I realized the impossibility of following Gilbert so closely that I could retain him in sight. In the first place, he would be inside a speeding taxi on his way to Milo's flat.

I halted with compressed lips. Was the call a hoax? Who had made it, anyway? It

28

was obviously made by someone who had seen Gilbert leaving the flats. For a moment I wrestled with the fantastic idea that the call might have been made by Hugh Maxwell.

I tried to dismiss all conjecture from my mind. I walked quickly along the road towards a taxi rank. I would drive to Milo's, tell Gilbert about the call. Hoax or not, I was determined he should know.

A taxi went slowly past me as I half-ran along the road. The driver leaned out.

'Taxi, Miss?'

I stepped off the pavement and went quickly towards the vehicle. He braked and stopped.

'Belmoir Court flats,' I said. 'Off the Bayswater Road.'

I sat back in the cab as the engine hammered noisily away. It was an old cab, but I sat staring ahead, seeing not the faded panels of the car but only fantastic visions of Gilbert in danger. There was danger, of that I was sure.

When I first looked through the taxi windows I was puzzled. Surely the driver was taking the wrong route to Bayswater?

I stared for a few minutes at flashing lights and passing cars and suddenly recognised a landmark. We had passed Charing Cross Station.

A few minutes later I glimpsed the Thames. I rapped on the glass panel behind the driver's head. He betrayed no interest, so in sudden anger I tried to open the taxi door

It was stuck, however. I tried the other side with no results. Then, as quick fear possessed me, I hammered furiously on the door handle. After an exasperating struggle the door was still fast shut, and I wondered how it had been possible for the driver to lock it without my knowledge. For it was locked, I was certain, and there were no windows, which would let down and so allow me to shout or wave to attract attention.

Suddenly I felt faint. There was some feeling of inescapable menace about the steady whirr of the tyres bearing me to some unknown destination. I watched streets slip by with a horrible feeling of futility made all the worse by the conviction that something was bound to happen to Gilbert.

The taxi sped on, past Cannon Street station and then on to the Mile End Road. I sat back, helpless and beset by anxieties. I realized now that the phone call was possibly a trap. This taxi had been waiting for me, knowing I would appear hurriedly seeking a cab. Why should anyone abduct me? Was Gilbert in danger?

And then the taxi slowed. I sat upright, scrutinising the locality. The driver turned his vehicle into a courtyard that seemed sandwiched between the high walls of dilapidated buildings. We stopped, and the driver climbed down. I sat tense. I was determined to scream and struggle the moment I got the chance.

The driver opened the door. A gun was in his hand. His peaked cap was over his eyes and the collar of his blue raincoat well turned up.

'If you make a sound or struggle, I'll rap you on the head with this butt,' he said evenly. 'I won't pretend that I'll shoot you, because we don't intend to go so far. Please get out!'

My plans evaporated under the quietly-delivered threat. I climbed down from the taxi. The man took my arm and we walked to a nearby door in the courtyard. It was dark and the air seemed suddenly chilly. I shivered. The door was opened by the man with the gun, and we went into a completely dark passage. I stumbled on some stairs.

'Keep right on,' said the man. 'Remember no harm will come to you if you do as you're told.'

'What do you want of me?' I asked quickly.

'You are a hostage,' was the brief reply.

At the top of the stairs I was ushered into a room. A light was burning from a gas jet, and a fire glowed. The room was meanly furnished with a bed, a table and two chairs and the curtains were drawn. There was one occupant.

Claudia stood near the fire, her hands thrust deep into her coat pockets, a mocking expression in her eyes.

'This is not quite so comfortable as Chelsea my dear, but you'll have to make do until your precious husband and

Victor Milo change their tune.'

'Claudia! What is the meaning of this? That phone call, who — ?'

'Don't worry, my pet, at the moment he is in no more danger than he can expect in his racket.'

'What do you mean — his racket?' I asked faintly. I felt nonplussed.

'What a sweet innocent!' Claudia sneered. 'It is time you knew your husband is the most unscrupulous agent Milo hires. Victor runs an extortion racket. Pay up or die, that is Victor's business rule, and I must say it pays — up-to-date. But it's risky.'

'How do you know all this?' I flung at her.

Claudia was not ruffled.

'Because I worked for Milo, up to a few hours ago. Now I quit. I'm going to be married. Safer, you see.'

'Aren't you afraid of Milo?' I retorted. 'Does he agree to your leaving him?'

'No, my dear Kathryn, Victor will not like it, but I'm through.'

'And so I'm a — hostage — !' I said. I stepped quickly across the room, the taxi driver watching me, gun in hand. With one hand I drew back the curtains round the window.

Iron bars across opaque glass met my eyes. I let the curtains fall.

'So this is a prison,' I said.

Claudia smothered a yawn.

'Definitely, my pet. But don't let it worry you.'

'Of course not,' I said grimly. 'But can you explain more? For instance, has this any connection with Gilbert's attack on you a few hours ago?'

Her eyes blazed. Beneath the heavy make-up, her facial muscles twitched in fury.

'You fair-haired bitch! I could ruin you! I could put Gilbert behind bars for a lifetime! And I will if he doesn't lay off Selby!'

Her voice rasped like that of any common woman of the street.

I said nothing more. We did not seem to be getting anywhere. I was a prisoner, and talking could not alter that. I wished I had a cigarette. If only I could do something incredible — something like the heroines on the screen who ask languidly for cigarettes, and then get hold of the gun. But I felt anything but languid. I was tense, ready to start at the slightest noise and ready to tremble with reaction afterwards.

Then I heard firm footsteps climbing the staircase outside. Claudia and the man with the gun turned their heads slowly.

The door opened and Hugh Maxwell walked in.

'You can put away that gun, Jack,' he said immediately. He came over and offered me a cigarette. I noticed his lighter functioned perfectly. Thankful for small mercies, I drew deeply at the cigarette, wondering what was to be revealed next.

All at once Claudia seemed to be in a hurry.

'I'm going, Maxwell,' she said. 'I've got to get some sleep, even if you seem able to do without it.'

'Jack will go with you,' said Hugh. 'After that idiotic scrap with Gilbert Brand, Milo will know you are a threat to him. You were a bit hasty, Claudia. I don't know why you couldn't have waited until we had our hostage.'

'I didn't wait,' said Claudia insolently, 'because it happened to be a personal affair between Brand and me.'

My throat seemed to tighten horribly.

'What — do — you — mean — Claudia?'

I swear there was contempt in her eyes. It stung me like a whip on the face. I had never known anything but laughter and friendship in other people's eyes. I felt as though I were seeing something repulsive.

'I mean, darling, that Gilbert was unreasonably annoyed when I teased him about my impending marriage to Jason Selby's son.'

I stared at her in a blurred way. I felt I must sit down — I must!

'Of course,' went on Claudia in her hard voice, 'as Maxwell will say, I was a bit hasty, but Gilbert had annoyed me. He cares too much for you, my pretty little girl, and I don't believe in playing second fiddle. A few months ago we met more than once, but that's all over. I'm marrying money, and Gilbert can go to the devil!'

'I'd like you to get out of here,' said Hugh harshly.

She smiled hastily.

'Be careful, Maxwell. She's pretty.'

And then they were gone. I was so dazed I did not realize they had left.

And then my senses cleared, with Hugh Maxwell sitting quietly by the fire staring at the coals. I felt I could not believe the things Claudia had said. I would not believe it! Gilbert loved me. There was no doubt about his love for me.

But it was merely reaction. Swift as a pendulum I swung to the other extreme and was wretched, knowing my life with Gilbert had fallen to fragments. My little bubble of happiness was floating out of my reach, and my pathetic hands could no more retrieve it than I could turn back time.

Hugh Maxwell said: 'Don't worry. Brand can hurt you, but that will pass.'

I gazed dumbly ahead, seeing little things, my cigarette almost burned to a thin chalk of ash, the shabby carpet,

Maxwell's brown shoes and heather-tweed suit.

'You'll have to stay here until Milo returns some documents to Denis Selby. That's the young fellow Claudia intends to marry. Milo will do it for Brand's sake — or our plan falls to the ground.'

I caught him watching me carefully with his dark eyes.

'Why don't you lie down?' he suggested.

'What are you going to do?' I asked.

'I'm staying here. I'm the only one who can be spared as guard. Jack Parsons — the taxi driver, you know — is contacting Gilbert Brand as soon as he returns to his flat.' Hugh gave his rare smile. 'Seems I'll have to sign on some new staff.'

'It was your idea to kidnap me?'

'No, Claudia's. She's the boss. She is paying my wages, and she sees that Denis Selby foots the bill. Denis is pretty soft. Claudia has determined to marry him, and I imagine she has him set. If you must know, Claudia is the driving force. Though I'm keen to smash Victor Milo, I can't do it for nothing. Claudia is interested only in money, and has arrived at the conclusion she could marry Denis Selby instead of being merely an instrument in the blackmail of his father.'

'And Victor Milo?' I asked automatically.

'He'll be annoyed. This is one way to get inside his armour. He runs a clever blackmailing organisation and works carefully. His victims are limited, and Milo does not try to hide behind masks or in darkened rooms when he contacts people. He has better methods than that. Anyone who squeals or rebels would simply be rubbed out by a paid gunman. It's the simplest, most effective way.'

'What will Milo do to Gilbert?' I asked suddenly.

'Gilbert Brand is Milo's chief lieutenant. Milo might dispense with him, but it is extremely unlikely.'

'So your scheme relies upon Gilbert influencing Milo to relinquish some hold upon Jason Selby,' I said wearily. 'And Claudia is double-crossing her former employer in order to marry the son of the man she helped to blackmail.'

'That's it.'

'Milo might rub you out — as he puts it,' I said harshly.

When he smiled again, I noticed the stern lines round his mouth.

'In all schemes of this nature,' he said, 'there are a score of 'ifs' and 'mights'. I usually keep my eyes on my chief motive. We are applying pressure to blackmailers.'

Blackmailer! The ugly word meant Gilbert! My handsome husband who had given me twelve months of sheer, thrilling life! If only my pleading would change him! Would Gilbert give up a crooked life? What would Gilbert do when he knew I was being used as a weapon against him?

And Hugh Maxwell was the type who would work to place Milo and Gilbert behind prison bars if he got the chance!

Hugh threw some pieces of coal on the fire, and then put an easy chair against the door. He lay down in the big seat with his raglan coat over his legs.

'Lie on the bed,' he advised. 'You'll feel better tomorrow. Don't try to get to this

40

door. It's locked, and I waken at the slightest movement.'

And he calmly closed his eyes.

I stood still for a long time. I saw a poker near the fire, and I toyed with the idea of using this to threaten him, but then I realized I simply couldn't. It seemed a fantastic situation. Here I was, a prisoner of a man who coolly went to sleep while guarding me. If only he had been brutal, I might have hated him sufficiently to use the poker, but as things were, I just could not bring myself to act. I stood helplessly, then wearily I approached the bed. I sat down, thinking, and in the stillness of the room the only sound was Maxwell's regular breathing. Was he asleep? Could I not escape and run pleading to Gilbert? These questions sickened my brain as they hurtled crazily round. I suddenly lay down.

I must have been asleep for some time when I awoke with a start.

A man was bending over me. His face was very close to me. I stared into Hugh Maxwell's dark eyes.

'You can go back to your chair,' I said

thinly, lying stiff, wary as a trapped animal.

He finished placing his coat around me.

'I thought you might feel cold,' he said. 'The fire is dying.'

And then he strolled back to the seat by the door, running his fingers through his dark hair. Slowly I relaxed.

I was so weary that sleep soon overtook me again. When next I awoke there were people in the room.

One was Jack Parsons. With his cap removed and his collar down, I could see he had the face of a prizefighter.

'I contacted Brand,' he was saying to Hugh Maxwell, 'and he intends to use his influence with Milo to get those papers returned to Jason Selby. Boy, that bloke was burning with fury!'

The other newcomer was a young man with a weak chin and brown, nervous eyes.

'I've had a phone call from Claudia,' he stammered to Hugh. 'She wants — er — she thinks it would be a good idea to be married tomorrow morning. Also, she thinks this room is not safe enough to hold this wretched girl, she feels she ought to be removed to Limmet's.'

'Limmet's!' Hugh Maxwell stiffened. 'It isn't necessary.'

'But Claudia insists!' protested the young man. 'She'll refuse to marry me if the girl is not removed immediately to Limmet's Home. Maxwell — it — it's an order!'

4

The Madhouse

Looking back I realize that Hugh
Maxwell was faced with an awkward
situation. He could not run his private
investigation agency without money, and
yet he was reluctant to give up the chance
of smashing Victor Milo. If he did not
accept Claudia's orders — and she was
behind the helpless Jason Selby and his
weak-kneed son — then Claudia might
dispense with his help.

I was sent along to Limmet's Home in
the old taxi.

It wasn't a long run, and in the dark
of the night, when I was hustled out of
the taxi, I could not be sure of my
whereabouts, but I had a feeling the place
was situated somewhere to the north of
the City.

Claudia had conceived a violent hatred
for me, I was sure, and she wanted to

make me suffer still more.

I was convinced of this when I realized Giles Limmet's Home was a lunatic asylum for women.

In the small office Hugh talked curtly to Limmet.

'Take every possible care of this girl. I don't wish her to be here, but Miss Jean Metcalfe will pay you, and these are her orders. I have no need to tell you to take care the police hear nothing of this.'

Limmet was a long shrivelled man with an expressionless face.

'She will come to no harm here,' he said.

I was taken to a room that was nothing more than a cell. Limmet attended to me personally. A table was brought in and a chair for my use. In one corner a canvas bed was placed.

'You won't be here long,' said Hugh. His eyes were grim.

And then I was alone.

I tried to settle, telling myself that Gilbert would act swiftly. He loved me, I was sure. He was a crook, but he would smash straight through this tangle.

I thought about Hugh Maxwell and his consideration for me. Meeting him anywhere else, I could imagine him being a grand friend.

And then my thoughts were interrupted by Giles Limmet. He unlocked the cell door.

'I've just received a phone call from Miss Metcalfe,' he stated, without a smile. 'She gives orders which are somewhat different from Mr. Maxwell's. Come with me.'

As I hesitated, he advanced and gripped my arms in a sudden peculiar hold. I realized this man was an expert in dealing with struggling women.

I was forced along a passage to a horrible, drab ward. It was rectangular in shape, with cold bare walls and a scrubbed floor. A number of beds were placed down one side, and sleeping forms lay on them. Even as I entered the ward, with Limmet holding my arms painfully, and a hard-faced woman in nurse's uniform standing by the door, I heard ghastly groans issue from the sleepers.

I was placed on a bed, and straps

quickly thrown over me. Within seconds I could not move a limb, and only my head was free. Awful mutterings and occasional crazy laughter came from the beds. I knew that some of the patients — prisoners would be a better description — were not asleep but actually strapped down.

'Why the change?' demanded the nurse.

Limmet said: 'I have orders that she is to be treated exactly as the others, with solitary confinement if she proves intractable.'

'What is her name?'

'She is a Brand,' said Limmet peculiarly.

The woman laughed disdainfully.

And then they withdrew. Limmet disappeared altogether, but the woman stayed, occasionally peering through a barred opening in the strong door.

A deep hatred of Claudia slowly grew inside me as I lay hour after hour in that ghastly ward. The crazy animal sounds of some of the poor souls round me grated on my nerves. I had no idea of the time. I lay waiting for the dawn to show through the barred windows on the other side of the wall. I tried to keep calm, telling myself that Gilbert would find me, that Hugh Maxwell would discover Claudia's trick and demand my release from these nerve-racking surroundings.

I could not sleep for my terror at some of the dreadful sounds that came to my ears. I stared into the semi-darkness and waited agonisingly for the long night to pass.

Somewhere among the dozen beds a woman moaned horribly and said: 'Gilbert!'

Every nerve in my body vibrated with terror. The voice said crazily: 'Gilbert!'

I was so tense that my body ached. I listened for a long terrible time and slowly my body relaxed from its painfully stiff tension.

The word was not repeated. I strained my neck muscles trying to identify the sleeper who had uttered the name so electrifying to me, but the strapped forms seemed all alike. I began to think my mind was playing tricks. Perhaps I had imagined the name was spoken!

Time dragged on and my eyes had

never closed. Then when dawn at last crept greyly into the ward, there was activity. Limmet and another nurse appeared, and the woman was as hard-faced as the one who had done duty all night. The patients were unstrapped and made to dress. I was released. I sat on the bedside, wondering if I could escape. I rubbed my stiff legs. I had been strapped down wearing my costume.

Apparently the inmates were to be paraded and taken away for breakfast. I watched some of them and shuddered. Poor crazy creatures! I wondered who had placed them in the hands of Limmet and his 'home'.

The woman attendant shouted 'Brand!'

I rose promptly enough and walked slowly forward. My lips were compressed, my hands clenched. I was determined to argue my way out of this beastly place.

Another woman walked uncertainly to the attendant. She had a pale, haunted face with a terrible scar running from her temple to her chin. For a brief second I thought, oddly enough, she had once been beautiful. Now her eyes were vacant, her movements childish.

'Not you!' said the woman attendant roughly, and with a strong motion of her hand held the mad woman back.

I walked on and the attendant followed me closely to the door. It was open and I passed through into a passage.

'Limmet wants to see you,' said the woman. 'Don't try any tricks with him. He keeps a cane in his office and if he uses it on you, you'll feel the welts for days, my girl.'

'A nice man!' I snapped.

Giles Limmet was having breakfast in his office when I entered.

'Sit down,' he said. 'You're having something to eat with me.'

And true enough I found myself looking at eggs and bacon, coffee, new bread. It was laid for me on the other side of his desk. 'Hurry up! Eat. Maxwell is coming over to see you, I guess,' said Limmet, and he gestured with his knife.

Recovering my confidence, I sat down. Despite my ghastly night, I felt hungry at the sight of food, and I began to eat.

'Aren't you afraid the police will close

you up?' I said quietly.

'No!' he said, somewhat surprised. 'We have nothing to hide.'

'Not much!' I muttered. I ate my breakfast. Soon afterwards Limmet's surmise proved correct. Hugh Maxwell was ushered into the office. The moment I saw him relief flooded through me. It was indescribable. Impulsively I ran to him. I clutched the tweed sleeves of his coat. My head was near his shoulder.

'Take me away from here, please! I've been strapped down in a horrible ward all night!'

His grip tightened. He said harshly to Limmet: 'Is that true?'

'Miss Metcalfe rang through with the order,' said Limmet. 'I take it she will pay the bill.'

'What was the idea?'

'Miss Metcalfe simply said she wished the girl to have no preferential treatment and to be placed among the other patients.'

Slowly Hugh ran his eyes contemptuously over Limmet.

'In future, so far as this girl is

concerned, you will take orders from me, Limmet.'

'Will you meet my fee if Miss Metcalfe refuses?'

'I will pay the fee,' said Hugh calmly, 'and make it reasonable, or I'll send the police along to examine the records of some of your patients.'

Limmet smiled nastily.

'I hope to send your husband along to collect you before the day is out,' said Hugh, turning to me, 'but it all depends upon Victor Milo. If he gives up some documents to Jason Selby, or his son, everything will be fine.'

'And what happens if Milo refuses?' I asked.

'He should not. And I'm relying upon Gilbert Brand's affection for you. I know his latest reaction: he is furious, and will undoubtedly do all he can to persuade Milo to give up the documents that enable him to blackmail Selby.'

As he spoke, Hugh Maxwell looked at me strangely.

'You still wish to return to your husband?' he went on.

'I do,' I said definitely. 'He is my husband. What else can I do?'

Hugh sighed. He fumbled for his cigarettes. He brought them out, and handed the case to me.

'I can see you will go back to him,' he muttered.

'I know he is a crook, and you would like to send him to jail,' I retorted bitterly, 'but as soon as I get the chance, I'm going to ask him to start a new life.'

I wondered why he threw his newly-lighted cigarette from him with an angry jerk.

'You little idiot. There will never be another life for Gilbert Brand. He is crooked through and through, and clever as blazes at that! I could tell you things about your own husband, my pretty little fool, that would horrify you. But I won't be the one to tell you! Brand will do that.'

At that, Giles Limmet laughed nastily.

'You are trying to frighten me,' I stammered.

I shall never forget the burning look in Hugh's eyes. Then I knew.

'I shall never do that,' he said, and his

lips hardly moved in his grim face.

Oh, he was half in love with me, I realized! The look in his eyes! What man can disguise his feelings when his eyes betray him? I understood now his consideration for me, the reason for this early visit. And, oh, there were a hundred other trivial things he had done and said.

While we were flinging these bitter words at each other, the telephone in Limmet's office rang. Limmet picked up the receiver. He spoke for a few seconds.

Then he handed the instrument to me.

'For you, Mrs. Brand,' he said softly.

I said 'Hello' into the mouthpiece.

'Hello, my pet,' said Claudia's mocking voice. 'Did you have a good night? Dream of your darling hubby, my dear?'

'You seem to be enjoying yourself, Claudia,' I said slowly.

'Well, I'm being married early today. Have you any advice to offer a bride? But then you're hardly a legitimate bride, are you?'

'Are you mad?' I snapped.

'Not in the slightest,' said Claudia. 'I am merely wondering if you met the real

Mrs. Brand last night. Limmet keeps her in a ward. Did you see her? She is absolutely raving mad, darling. Gilbert could tell you an interesting story about his real wife — for they were never divorced!'

5

Revenge Against Claudia

I never remembered replacing the receiver. I do know I laughed jerkily, uncontrollably.

Claudia's taunts were absolutely unreal to me. A thin metallic voice had glibly spoken words that should have seared my mind.

'It was Claudia,' I said mechanically to Hugh. 'She — said — Gilbert — has a wife — mad — mad!'

'She's been here two years,' said Giles Limmet simply, with an evil grin.

And then I remembered the woman who had moaned 'Gilbert' during the night. I had a swift stark remembrance of the pale woman who moved forward when the attendant called 'Brand'.

Then the world rocked and everything went black.

When I recovered I was lying on a settee in Limmet's office, and Hugh was bending anxiously over me. I had swooned completely. This had never happened to me before in my strong young life. But the sledgehammer realization of Gilbert's wickedness, following on a sleepless, harrowing night, had affected me too much.

'Drink this hot coffee,' muttered Hugh.

'It is true — about Gilbert?'

He nodded. His fine eyes were full of pity. I really believe Hugh Maxwell would have killed anyone who, at that moment, had hurt me further.

'You had to learn soon,' he said. 'I had hoped Gilbert Brand would tell you himself and that you could somehow thrash the matter out between you. I learnt about this when I entered the case and sought for means of fighting Victor Milo and Brand. I found out that Brand's wife was mad and maintained at Limmet's Home. Unfortunately, Claudia was with me when I made the first routine investigation. She is clever. She realized this was a weapon against Brand. At first she wanted to use the discovery to apply pressure to Brand so that Selby's documents could be recovered. She is determined to marry Denis

Selby. The youngster has plenty of money, and is completely infatuated with her. I tried to make her forget about Brand's wife, but she never has. I think she hates you ever since Brand nearly strangled her at Milo's party. She had taunted him about his mad wife, taunted him about you and the fact that she was marrying Denis Selby. Brand did not get the chance to inform Milo about Claudia's double-cross while he was with you, but he would undoubtedly do so when he returned to Milo's last night. By that time Claudia had left.'

He had spoken in a calm, rapid voice. But one fact stood out with horrible significance.

'My marriage with Gilbert is not real — it is bigamous!' I gasped.

'I could put him behind bars for that alone,' said Hugh sternly. 'He would get a few months. But that would not break him and Milo. And my job is to protect my client, Selby.'

'How is it Gilbert's' — I choked — 'wife is mad?'

Hugh explained quietly. 'She was a very beautiful woman when they were married

58

four years ago and, unlike you, she married him with her eyes wide open. In other words, she knew Brand was a crook. Roberta was not a criminal type herself, but soon adjusted herself to Brand's life without complaint. Then came an accident. Gilbert was driving his car to meet a certain man — it was before he lined up with Milo — and another equally determined scoundrel, from whom Brand had hijacked some jewels, was following closely. With Brand was his wife. The car piled up on a bend and Gilbert had a miraculous escape, but not so Roberta. She spent a long time in an expensive nursing home, which suited Brand because of the privacy, but she never recovered her sanity. She bears a scar along her face as a result of the accident.'

I held my head and saw only the pale woman with the scar. I rose abruptly to my feet.

'How much longer must I stay here?' I cried.

Hugh looked grim, unhappy.

'I have told you I think you'll get away today — if Brand succeeds in influencing

Milo. Brand thinks a great deal about you,' said Hugh bitterly. 'He will be here.'

'But I can't stay here! I'll go mad!'

'There is no other place I can take you. Claudia insists I take no chances.'

'She is your boss!' I flung at him.

'She is right, in a way. Milo and Brand are dangerous men. We have played our hand. Milo would send his hired men to rub me out or get rid of Claudia or even threaten Denis Selby. Only with you as hostage can I prevent anything like that happening.'

And so Hugh was forced to leave me. I was taken back to the small room and locked in. I sat on the chair with my head and arms resting on the table. I was in a dark, tortured mood. I could not bear to think of Gilbert, yet my thoughts dwelt on the incredible fact that I was not really his wife.

For twelve glorious months the fact that we were married had been my most cherished knowledge. I had been so proud of our happy-go-lucky marriage!

And now my dream-life was utterly ruined, and all I could cling to was the belief that I still loved Gilbert and he loved me.

In that small room the hours dragged like years. Twice during the day a woman brought meals. I could hardly taste them. I was waiting — waiting for Gilbert or for my freedom to go to him.

At last, after the woman had brought me a frugal tea, Hugh Maxwell entered with Gilbert.

I ran to the man I loved. While his arms held me tight, I trembled violently. I looked into his eyes and saw they were frighteningly blue and narrowed. A little muscle twitched on his smooth cheek.

'Take care of her, Brand,' said Hugh Maxwell, unemotionally.

'I won't forget you for this,' said Gilbert thickly. He added: 'I'll remember Claudia especially.'

Hugh was silent.

I stammered out: 'Oh, Gilbert! We have so much to talk about! Take me home! Please!'

Giles Limmet was present. It was he who said: 'Aren't you wanting to see Roberta, Mr. Brand?'

He was malicious. Inside that long shrivelled body there was a vicious streak of cruelty.

Gilbert snapped: 'No! And keep your cursed mouth shut, Limmet!'

We went out to a waiting taxi. As the car drove off, I caught a glimpse of Hugh leaving Limmet's Home. His face was inscrutable.

Gilbert told me a great deal during the ride back to Chelsea. He spoke, in curt, grim sentences, realizing I knew everything and that it was futile for him to pretend any longer. He said Victor Milo had been angry and obstinate, and that he had had to give promises that bound him more and more to the man. Only then had Milo consented to release some mysterious documents that Jason Selby anxiously desired.

'Milo had bought these papers from another man who had once been a business partner of Selby, and the papers proved Selby was once guilty of fraudulent conversion,' said Gilbert. 'Milo gave them to me and I handed them to Maxwell. If I'd known he'd detained you at Limmet's I'd have seen him in Hades before he got those papers. I'd have got you away from Limmet's easily.'

I remembered Hugh saying Milo and Gilbert could hire gunmen, and terror clawed at my heart.

'Gilbert, you must break away from Milo!' I cried.

'It is utterly impossible.'

'Please — for my sake! Oh, Gilbert, for your own, if you like! Maxwell is out to smash you.'

'If Maxwell crosses me again,' he hissed, 'I shall kill him.'

He leaned back, and there was murder in his eyes. He added in an even grimmer tone: 'I have not forgotten Claudia, either!'

I clenched my hands. In trying to reform Gilbert and straighten our lives. I was apparently attempting to move mountains.

I shall not forget that night at the flat when I faced the stark realization that I could not stay with Gilbert any longer. Our marriage was bigamous and re-marriage was impossible so long as his wife lived or he remained undivorced.

This, then, was the sordid end to my beautiful twelve months! I did not weep, but it was only because of an immense effort at self-control.

'You *could* stay,' snapped Gilbert.

'Please, Gilbert! Let's save at least our self-respect from the wreck!'

His strong arms bound me. He tilted my face and kissed me for a long time. I did not even try to slip away. I let him kiss me, and I wondered why the thrill had vanished.

I looked into his sombre eyes.

'I'll stay,' I said, trembling, 'if you promise faithfully to give up crime.'

He could have glibly promised, but he would not stoop so low to me.

'It won't work,' he said harshly. 'We are living at the rate of thousands a year. I could not earn that much except by contact with men like Milo — or on my own. I'm crooked, Kathryn, and you might as well know it. What are you going to do?'

The blood was drained from my face. I felt it.

'I shall see you every day,' I said faintly. 'I shall never give up trying and hoping.'

'I won't let you go.'

I tried to laugh. 'But you must. We'll find a way out.'

Automatically I packed some of my clothes. I phoned a nearby hotel and reserved a room. Gilbert watched me, smoking deeply all the time.

'I suppose Claudia married her choice today,' I commented casually.

'She's married trouble,' said Gilbert cryptically.

'Will she sing again at the Superb?' I chattered.

'If Milo decides, she'll never sing again.'

I grabbed his arm. 'You must stop speaking that way!' I said earnestly.

He merely smiled.

Some time later I was installed in the modest hotel which offered me a splendid little bedroom and bathroom. I made my way down to the lounge where I had arranged to meet Gilbert over a sherry.

But as time flew by and I sat waiting, I knew that Gilbert was not coming. I was on the point of rising, determined to visit the flat and see him, when Hugh Maxwell walked into the lounge.

He came along and sat down at the little table beside me.

'So you have left Brand?'

'In a sense,' I replied.

I knew he understood.

'You are not tied to him anyhow,' he said calmly, as if speaking to himself. 'You are free to marry. You were never really married to him.'

I flushed, and he bit his lip.

'I'm speaking plainly because I want to make myself clear,' he went on. 'I see no reason why you shouldn't marry again.'

I retorted as coolly as he: 'Whom do you suggest I marry?'

'You could marry me.'

He spoke unemotionally, but I was startled. Then, suddenly, his dark eyes were flooded with feeling.

'If you marry me, Brand will not pester you, and, furthermore, and this is important, Milo would be unable to get at you. I would see to that.'

'Does Milo want to get at me?'

'Yes, he is planning to bind Gilbert more strongly to his side and will threaten to have you locked away if Gilbert does not carry out orders.'

'He couldn't do that!' I gasped.

'He could. Milo is also planning vengeance against Claudia as a pleasant sideline.'

'How do you know this?'

'Well, it is quite simple,' Hugh said. 'Actually Milo rang me up just after I got back to my office. He boasted a bit in that menacing way of his. He is a typical criminal type. He did not say what his plans were against Claudia.'

Hugh caught the eye of a waiter, and ordered a sherry and a whisky.

'Will you marry me?' he asked.

And I said quietly, as if the whole thing were not quite fantastic: 'It's impossible. I could only marry one man and — he — is married already.'

'Victor Milo will have you in his power along with Gilbert if you stay in London.'

'Perhaps I could commission you to protect me,' I said.

'I am doing that — Kathryn,' he replied softly.

I had to lower my eyes.

'I am also working for Claudia, who is certainly worried now. She has had a bad attack of nerves. She is afraid of Milo,' he said.

'On her wedding night,' I murmured. 'If she is not leaving London, I hope she enjoys her honeymoon.'

'She is not leaving. Denis Selby is attending to his father's business; the old man is ill.'

I looked round the lounge fretfully, hoping against fading hope that Gilbert would appear.

'If you are looking for Gilbert,' said Hugh, 'I can tell you he has gone to see Milo, on Milo's sudden order.'

Worry shot through my eyes.

'How do you know?'

'My assistant, Jack Parsons, trailed him and phoned the information to me.'

'I hate Milo,' I said savagely. 'That man will crash down and bring Gilbert with him. I wonder why he wanted to see Gilbert?'

'Probably to talk over schemes. Possibly to intimate to Gilbert how much he can hurt him by threatening you. And possibly, for it is the most immediate of Milo's ambitions, they are talking of ways and means to get even with Claudia.

'Aren't you anxious to protect your client?'

'Yes. And I'm anxious to see Brand and Milo go to jail. They'll make a slip yet.'

'I am going out,' I said determinedly, and I rose.

I left Hugh and went to my room. I changed quickly into a dark, pin-stripe costume and put on my sealskin coat. I did not bother about a hat.

As I crossed the lobby on the hotel, Hugh Maxwell stepped up to me again.

'If you are going to see Gilbert at Milo's place, I'm going with you,' he said.

'But I don't need you. Please!'

All my arguments, however, were useless. He was determined, and in the end I found myself sitting inside a taxi with him.

Outside the Bayswater block, which housed Milo's flat we met Jack Parsons, Hugh's pugilistic assistant. The man touched the brim of his slouch hat as he looked at me.

'I wondered if you'd be along, Mr. Maxwell. There's a party on. Brand left with two men who were city-bred toughs, or I don't know what I'm talking about.'

'Which direction did they take?'

'They went west, towards Uxbridge Road.'

'This is it,' said Hugh. He glanced doubtfully at me.

'You'll have to go back to your hotel.'

'I want to know where Gilbert has gone. Do you know where he is going?'

'Yes,' said Hugh, brutally. 'He is going to kill Claudia Selby.'

For a moment the street rocked about me, but I quickly recovered.

'You are making wild guesses!' I flung at him.

'Perhaps, but this is a guess based on pretty sound reasoning. Jack, get two taxis. Mrs. — er — Brand is returning to her hotel.'

'You are wasting your money,' I said coolly. 'I shall simply order my driver to follow your cab.'

And then he laughed shortly. He shouted to the departing Jack: 'Better get hold of one taxi.'

Presently Jack returned from a rank further down the road.

He opened the door of the taxi, and we climbed in and were off in a matter of seconds.

But it was an agonising journey to me. Thinking of Gilbert going to do murder was a horror only too real. Milo had commanded it. Milo was now all-powerful, a revengeful desperate criminal with Gilbert in his clutches completely.

I believed everything Hugh said. It all fitted in so terribly and logically.

After a longish journey, the taxi stopped in a dark lane, well into the suburbs. Hugh and Jack Parsons descended, and Hugh tried to persuade me to stay inside the taxi.

'You must stay here,' he said. He shouted to the driver: 'See that this lady does not leave the cab. It is for her own safety.'

The man looked startled but nodded an assent.

But my mind was made up, and when Hugh and Jack departed I quickly slipped out on the other side of the taxi and heard a plaintive shout as I raced quickly into the dark night taking the same direction as the two men. The driver shouted to me to stop, but I ran in haste along the shade of a high stone wall over which tall trees frowned. It was pitch dark but I was sure Hugh had gone this way because there was no other turning, and I hoped to find the Selby house.

I had some vague idea of stopping Gilbert in his dreadful intention.

And then I blundered into the fight.

Five men were struggling near a wide iron gate, and with sickening fears I recognized Gilbert, Hugh and Jack Parsons among them. Two other men were flailing fists at Hugh and Jack. The dull sound of nauseating blows came to my ears. On the ground lay the body of a woman.

Claudia! Was she dead?

Like a fool I ran towards the men. I disregarded Claudia. I shrieked at Gilbert and then at Hugh. I raised my fists and struck ineffectively at one of the unknown men, He seemed not to notice me, but redoubled his attacks on Hugh.

And then I noticed the wicked, hard rubber blackjacks in the hands of the two unknown men. Hugh and Jack were fighting savagely, but they were two to three. All at once I saw Jack go down and realized that the blackjacks had been used.

Three men crowded round Hugh, and the end came suddenly. His unconscious body fell beside Jack's. One of the thugs kicked violently at him as he fell. I screamed in fear.

They turned on me, and Gilbert's face was furious.

'You, Kathryn!'

He stopped one of the thugs from leaping at me.

'Get Claudia over your shoulder,' I heard him rasp.

The man obeyed.

Then came the sound of voices and running footsteps on the drive leading to the iron gate.

'Maxwell's other men!' snapped Gilbert. 'Get along to the car!'

He grabbed my hand and ran me

madly along the road.

There, in a small garage runway, lay a car. I was bundled in and the engine murmured with subdued power. Another second and the car shot down the road.

6

Gilbert Suggests A New Start

'Your wedding day has sure proved a flop, Claudia,' sneered Victor Milo.

She had been unconscious and was now sitting defiantly in a chair with her legs and hands bound with black adhesive tape wrapped round four or five times.

The car had brought us swiftly to this cellar, but where the place was situated I had not the faintest idea. During the swift reckless journey my mind had been fogged with horror. I was not sure that Claudia lived. She had lain so limply on the floor of the back seat of the big car that I supposed she had been killed. One of the thugs watched me like a vulture watching its prey. Gilbert drove the car swiftly, expertly.

And then I had been hustled from the car into a door hardly a yard away. We went down stone stairs to the cellar and found Milo waiting.

One of the thugs departed on some errand, and the other remained, acting as a sort of attendant. Milo called him Lemuel.

I saw Claudia shiver, and it was not only because her dress was torn and too thin to resist the earthy damp, which rose from the cellar floor. Hating her for the things she had done to me, I could yet pity her now she was in the power of Victor Milo, for what his intentions were I was soon to learn.

'You're not so smart as you think, Claudia,' he commented. 'You spoilt a good deal of mine when you hired Maxwell and married Selby, but now you're in a spot I'll get my money out of young Selby — I'll hold you to ransom Claudia. What do you think of that?'

'I think Maxwell will get you soon,' she retaliated.

Milo shrugged his immense shoulders. The gesture showed the Latin in his makeup, that and his love of rings; though his white, soft face was not typically Latin.

'Gilbert tells me Maxwell had two men at your house as protection. They must have been mugs. Think you're worth five thousand pounds to Denis Selby, Claudia?' Milo made the inquiry in a suave voice.

She was silent and unafraid. Her eyes flashed venom at him.

'If Selby decides your value is not so high, you will disappear,' added Milo. Suddenly his voice betrayed stark viciousness. 'Either way will give me my revenge.'

He turned to me. I tried to stare calmly into his glittering black eyes.

'Do you know you cost me a hundred a week?' he asked

'Perhaps Gilbert serves you well enough for that amount,' I retorted.

'Sure. He's a good boy. He knows the best people, and guys like that are hard to get. Now, why have you left him?'

'He has a wife living.'

The white face smiled contemptuously.

'Why should you worry? You'll stick to him in future, and if he doesn't keep in line with me, he'll suddenly lose you.'

'You needn't direct your threats at her, Milo,' said Gilbert harshly.

'No?' Milo swung to Lemuel. 'You've got a job, Lem. Look after Claudia. Don't paw her, and watch for tricks. She hasn't to leave this cellar. You'll be relieved at intervals, until Denis Selby pays up.'

Victor Milo brought out a large clean handkerchief from his jacket pocket. His eyes met mine.

'We're leaving by a different route, and you'll have to be blindfolded. You have no objection, Gilbert?' he inquired with exaggerated politeness.

Gilbert shook his head briefly. I stood still while the white handkerchief was tied tightly across my eyes.

I was taken up the stone stairs with Gilbert behind me, steadying me with one hand. Now and then he muttered a word of reassurance. Milo, I knew, was leading the way.

And then as I walked confidently enough in total darkness with Gilbert's hand pressing on my back, I heard the unmistakable scurry and squeaking of rats on the floor immediately ahead of me.

I started like a frightened animal. Perhaps I shouted out. At all events I instinctively ran to one side. Gilbert's touch was too light to hold me, and the next moment I blundered into some solid object. I hurt my leg and stumbled.

Strong hands helped me to my feet, and at the same time I realized the bandaging handkerchief had partially slipped.

I could see the dim shape of the big hall-like building we were traversing. I remained silent, and wondering if Milo or Gilbert had noticed the handkerchief was not quite in position.

As my eyes grew accustomed to the light, I saw we were in a large warehouse stacked with an amazing variety of theatrical props. I saw screens, wooden statues, ropes, canvases and boxes of all sizes. I was taken across this storage warehouse to a small wicket door, but I took care not to be too careful in avoiding the obstructions.

A big car stood immediately outside this door. Gilbert ushered me into the rear seat, while Milo locked the wicket door behind us. But there was time for me to take one swift glance at my surroundings. Directly ahead loomed the three tall chimneys of a factory, and the light from the newly-risen moon fell wanly upon a great white sign: *Lemer's Metalwork & Castings*. And as I sat back in the car, I knew that I had provided myself with a key to the whereabouts of Milo's headquarters — and Claudia's prison!

Milo drove off, and after a few minutes Gilbert was given orders to take the handkerchief from my eyes. I thought a little convincing acting would not come amiss at this stage. I quickly rubbed my eyes, and complained of the tightness of the bandage. Gilbert kissed me, and Milo gave a satisfied chuckle.

Gilbert took me back to my hotel in Chelsea.

'Why fool around like this?' he demanded. 'Why can't you return to the flat?'

'We've discussed that, Gilbert,' I said wearily.

'Don't be a fool! Roberta is dead to the world. I wish she was dead!'

And now his narrowed eyes did not charm me. I was frightened.

I turned from him, and ran up to my room.

I knew what I had to do. It was nothing less than common humanity, although I could never forgive Claudia for the spiteful things she had done to me. Still, I could not allow her to be confined in a cellar with some awful fate hanging over her if her husband refused to negotiate with Victor Milo. And then I had a desire to strike a blow at Milo.

I went down into the lounge later and put a call through to Hugh Maxwell's Holborn office. As I expected I could get no reply. I searched the directory for Jason Selby's telephone number, and when I found it, I went ahead with the call.

At first I spoke to Denis Selby, and I sensed the young man was nearly distracted. Then Hugh came to the phone.

'I can tell you where to find Claudia,' I said. 'But, tell me, are you badly hurt?'

'Just a few bruises,' was the reply. 'Why didn't you stay in the taxi?'

'Because I don't take orders from you, Mr. Maxwell,' I said coolly.

'Gilbert and his thugs were lucky,' said

Hugh rapidly. 'Where is Claudia?'

'In a theatrical depository near a factory in the suburbs, a place called 'Lemer's Metalworks & Castings'.' I paused while he repeated the names. 'Milo intends to demand five thousand pounds ransom or Claudia disappears. At the moment there is only one guard over Claudia.'

'Thanks, we'll find the place. Are you now in Milo's confidence that he reveals his hideouts to you?'

'I was blindfolded but the handkerchief slipped,' I said quietly. 'I hope you will help me with Gilbert when the time arrives.'

'You could help yourself by forgetting the swine completely,' was the harsh answer I received.

I slipped out of the telephone enclosure and was passing the fire in the lounge when Gilbert swiftly walked towards me.

I had no idea he was still in the hotel, and I stared, surprised.

'Who were you phoning?' he demanded.

'A friend,' I replied quickly.

'Why?'

'I intend to leave town for a few days,' I said quietly.

He seemed to hesitate. Then: 'I've made up my mind, Kathryn. I'm quitting Milo. I want you to come with me. I'll give up everything crooked, and get into business. I mean it, Kathryn. I'll go straight for you. We could get out of the country — go to America or France!'

I was so surprised that I could not speak. He went on urgently: 'You said you'd go with me if I promised to go straight.'

'Yes, I said that!' I agreed mechanically.

'Well, this is it. I've been thinking everything over. I can't go on living without you. It's stalemate, and I give way, my dear.'

Still, I was numb with the unexpected development. Then slowly I realized what it all meant.

'What of — your — real wife?' I stammered.

'She will be looked after. Kathryn, you promised you'd go with me if I gave up Milo.'

I must have been white-faced. I had made the promise, but I was just realizing what it meant. I would not be Gilbert's real wife. The old magic of our life together could not be maintained with haunting memories of the scarred woman shut up in Limmet's Home.

Yet I had promised, and, heaven knows, I still loved Gilbert. Even if our old carefree manner of living had vanished, it would be a great thing to get him out of a life of crime. If I kept my promise, Gilbert would keep his.

'I'll go with you,' I said at last, and I leaned towards him before I realized we were standing in the lounge of a hotel. 'But what will Milo do? Won't he be furious?'

'I have a plan. It happens I can get reservations on a plane leaving tomorrow morning for Paris, although the price is pretty devilish. After we land in Paris, we can make arrangements to fly to America. Milo has a great many activities which will keep him tied down in this country for some time, so once we get away everything will be fine.'

I looked deeply into those blue eyes.

'Gilbert, why have you so suddenly changed your mind?'

'Because I love you, Kathryn.'

I cannot explain exactly, but his whispered words did not thrill me as they would have done in the old days. Perhaps I was worried. In truth, I had enough to worry me.

'Be packed by 10 o'clock tomorrow morning,' he said. 'I'll call for you.'

And with that he left me.

I should have been full of new hope, but I somehow felt subdued. And yet this was what I had wanted — to see Gilbert begin a new life. Of course, I knew what was wrong. Our marriage was no longer real and true.

I sat for nearly three-quarters of an hour in the lounge, thinking, and, when the other residents were beginning to retire for the night, I went to the phone once more. I wanted to learn if Claudia had been rescued.

I got through to the Selbys' house because it seemed more likely that Hugh Maxwell would return there with Claudia.

I waited a few moments after speaking to a servant, and then I heard Hugh's voice.

'We've just got back. Everything went like clockwork. Milo's man was surprised to see us raid that cellar. He didn't have much chance against four men, though we had to knock him out. Claudia is back with her husband.'

'I'm glad,' I said in a low voice.

'I've told her she has to thank you.'

'It's all right,' I said.

'I'm worried about you. Milo will start thinking, and he's shrewd. He'll not be happy until he learns how news of his secret hideout leaked out so quickly.'

'Oh, everything is going to be all right,' I said.

'Do you think so?' he replied, doubtfully. 'I shouldn't underrate Milo. Why don't you get away from London? Better still, marry me and I'll protect you to the finish.'

'It is very gallant of you to offer yourself,' I said softly. He said nothing for a moment and then replied, and I could almost imagine the feeling flooding his fine eyes, 'I'm asking you because I want you — and some day I'll get you.'

I said hurriedly: 'Please don't talk like

that. If — if — you want to know — and you should — I'm leaving London with Gilbert tomorrow. He's cutting away from Milo and going straight. I — I — hope you understand.'

I heard him say, 'I see,' slowly. Then the line went dead.

I went to my room and, throwing myself on the bed, soon fell asleep — into the deep, dreamless sleep of exhaustion.

In the morning I was terribly hungry and ate a good breakfast. I regarded this as a good omen. My appetite was back to normal, so perhaps my worries were vanishing.

I packed, humming a popular song as I did so. Gilbert was making a fresh start, so why shouldn't all the other nagging worries be solved some day? Time and patience would effect everything. Some day Gilbert and I would be happy again.

Then I thought of the woman with the haunted, vacant face and my song stopped. All at once I felt depressed and sick at heart.

Later, I met Gilbert in the lounge. He was spruce in a new suit, but his face was angry. He took my arm and led me to a secluded recess.

'Claudia got away last night,' he said, and his lips hardly moved.

I tried to smile.

'Need we worry about that? It's Milo's concern now, dear.'

'You're not surprised,' he accused. 'And it's more than Milo's concern.'

'But Gilbert — how — I — what is wrong?'

'I was after that five thousand pounds,' snarled Gilbert. 'Milo had assigned me to collect — on his behalf. But I had other ideas.'

'What do you mean?'

'I mean I intended to get the money from the Selby fool this morning and get away with it to Paris. I need that blasted money!'

'You'd double-cross Milo! You'd take ransom money!' I nearly choked on the words.

'Do you think we can travel and live on nothing?' asked Gilbert in a furious low whisper.

'I — I — have some money!'

'I tell you it is not enough. We can't go to Paris now. I was banking on that cursed five thousand. That was part of the idea. Now you've spoilt it.'

'I — spoilt — it!' I stammered.

'Yes. Don't look so confoundedly stupid! You know as well as I do that you tipped Maxwell about the cellar at the warehouse.'

'I . . . I — !' I tried to defend myself. Cold fear was creeping up my spine.

'It must have been you. *It could be no one else.* Milo will soon come to the same conclusion, even if he does not now understand how you knew where to send Maxwell. You've put me on the spot, Kathryn.'

7

I Talk To Milo

I ran from Gilbert and went to my room where I sat in a chair, my hands clenched, my gaze fixed unseeingly on the wall ahead.

One thing was very clear; Gilbert's intentions to reform had not been very deep. Even while he had talked of going straight, he had planned to steal the ransom money from Milo.

What would have happened after we reached Paris?

I did not want to think. I stood up and paced the floor. And then my thoughts nagged at me again. Did Gilbert really love me? Was his anger the result of concern on my behalf? Or was he afraid, now that he had failed to get the five thousand, of offending Victor Milo?

I hated the idea of brooding any more upon my troubles. I left the hotel, determined to see Hugh Maxwell, and in a sudden fit of economy went by underground.

I thought the wisest course was to visit his Holborn office. I was still dressed in the clothes in which I had expected to travel with Gilbert. I had a lovely little hat perched on my head, I suppose a man might think it absurd, but it did suit my fair hair. Under my coat I wore a crimson dress, which, I thought wryly, befitted me in the circumstances under which I had hoped to go to Paris with Gilbert. Sheer silk stockings and court shoes completed the ensemble. I wondered vaguely what the effect would be on Hugh Maxwell.

I came out of the tube at Holborn and walked along seeking Carter Street. I paused at the corner when I found the thoroughfare, looking at the numbers, while a continual stream of people passed to and fro.

Then, very quietly, a man attached himself to me. He was of medium height and clad in a cheap suit and hat.

'Don't attract attention,' he said, spitting out each word and taking my arm. 'I'm holding a hypodermic syringe to your arm. Now — !'

I jerked in spite of his warning.

'Be still!' he snapped. 'Or I'll give you the dose. When you collapse, I'll tell people you're my friend and you've fainted. Then I'll put you in a taxi. Or are you going to be quiet?'

'You're from Milo, I suppose?'

'That's right. You're going to see him. By taxi, when I get one. Don't make a row. I've done worse jobs than this, sister.'

He seemed grimly confident. He held my arm tightly and yet casually, using two hands, and we walked along together.

Amazing as it seemed, I was being kidnapped in broad daylight in a crowded London street. Yet, as I thought hard, there was no reason why the man should not use the hypodermic concealed in the palm of his hand. If I showed the slightest sign of resistance he would give me 'the dose' as he called it. Then he would have the cool nerve to claim me as his friend and place me in a taxi.

As it was, he had the usual luck of his kind, for a taxi came cruising along. He hailed it, and within seconds I was reluctantly climbing into the vehicle. The driver received his muttered instructions and drove off.

'Milo had a row with Gilbert this morning,' said my captor. 'Milo wanted to see you, but Gilbert refused to bring you over. So I guess the boss will be glad I've got you. I was getting sick of hanging round Maxwell's place.'

'Gilbert Brand will thrash the life out of you when he hears about this,' I retorted.

'Yeah? Well, you're no asset to Gilbert Brand, and he ought to get wise!'

I sat back, controlling my anger. I was not afraid. Milo would surely not dare to harm me. Even if we had quarrelled, Gilbert would not allow that.

The taxi penetrated more deeply into the Soho district, and eventually stopped before a small café of a poor type. I was taken through the sparsely-populated restaurant to a back room, my guide exchanging nods with a greasy proprietor standing beside a counter.

After going through a passage, my

93

escort knocked at a door, and after a considerable pause, a voice bade us enter.

Milo was evidently in conference with one of his underlings, but when we entered the foreign-looking individual left at a jerk from Milo's head.

'What have you been up to, Dave?' snapped Milo. 'Where did you find her? Who told you to bring her along?'

'I thought you'd be glad!'

'Thought! Who the devil told you to think? Your orders were to watch Maxwell's movements for the next three hours.'

'But you wanted to see this skirt, boss. I heard you say so!'

'Sure. Are you certain you attracted no attention?'

'It was easy for me, Milo,' boasted Dave.

'Then get to blazes out of here! Get back to watching Maxwell.'

Dave scuttled out of the room, closing the door carefully after him. Milo scrutinised his nails.

'You know, I'm beginning to think you're a nuisance to me and to Brand.'

'Indeed,' I replied.

'Yes, particularly after last night. Maxwell found his way to that cellar very easily, and within an hour of our leaving Lemuel on guard. Pretty good going, I guess. How did you know where to send Maxwell?'

'I didn't send him,' I lied reluctantly.

Milo rose with smouldering eyes. He came purposefully towards me.

'You pretty little snake! That's the second racket you've spoilt. I think I'll spoil your beauty — like this!'

His ringed hand smacked against my cheek. Pain jerked tears to my eyes. I put up my hand and felt blood on my face.

'If I mussed you up, maybe Gilbert might forget you and be a darned sight more useful to me,' he said cruelly.

Deliberately he brought a horrible-looking brass knuckleduster from his pocket and slipped it on his hand. He drew back his fist.

At that moment the door opened and Gilbert walked in.

I had shrunk back against the wall, but, on seeing Gilbert, I slipped over to him.

'Take me away from here, Gilbert,' I cried. 'Oh, take me away!'

'I thought I left you at your hotel!'

'They kidnapped me!' I gasped.

Milo rammed his hand in his pocket. 'Sure. And, now you two are here, you can listen to me.' Milo faced Gilbert, an implacable expression in his dark eyes. 'Your girl messed up last night's job. She's causing me trouble, Gilbert, and I don't like it. I want a guarantee there'll be no more trouble from her. Can you give it?'

'There'll be no more trouble, Milo,' said Gilbert quickly.

'That's fine. You know it costs money to hire men and when the job flops there is a dead loss. That's why you can't start on your own, Gilbert. You've got no money.'

There was mockery in the drawled words. Gilbert remained silent his face dark. To change Milo from this mocking tone I tumbled out the first thought that entered my head.

'He hit me, Gilbert!'

Gilbert gave a curt, imperceptible nod.

I realized he had seen the blood on my cheek and guessed why it was there.

Milo had struck me, but Gilbert was unmoved!

It was then that my calmness deserted me.

'Oh, Gilbert, won't you give this up? Please get away from all this! You could do it! Gilbert — you promised me you'd break away today!'

And then I stopped, aghast at the significance of my outburst.

Milo gave Gilbert a penetrating gaze before walking slowly across the room. Reaching a chair, he lowered his bulk to its support and then looked up at Gilbert. His black eyes were bleak. Gilbert stood motionless. I flashed a fearful glance at him, wondering at his calm self-control.

'Take her away, Gilbert,' said Milo tonelessly. 'Just go home. I may want you later.'

To me his ordinary words seemed full of ominous meaning. There was menace in every gentle syllable.

But Gilbert accepted the directions quietly.

He led me out of the room to the café, and only then did he speak.

'What the devil made you blather like that?'

'I — I — didn't think.'

'Obviously, my dear Kathryn. I suppose you don't realize that Victor Milo is one of the most dangerous men in London? I'll have to convince him you're a little fool, and didn't realize what you were saying.'

'Gilbert, please don't talk to me like that!'

'You practically force me to. And what is more, you'll have to return to the flat. I've given my guarantee to Milo that you won't cause more trouble.' He sneered. 'You seem too fond of making calls upon Hugh Maxwell, my Kathryn!'

In the end, after a lot of argument, I went with Gilbert to the flat, but I firmly intended going to my hotel as soon as night came. I was worried about Gilbert, however. I knew my tongue had blundered in talking wildly about his leaving Milo. I had an instinctive feeling that Milo would attempt to impress on Gilbert the rashness of such a move.

The hours at the flat passed in strained attempts by me to engage Gilbert in conversation. For a long time he stared moodily out of the window at the traffic passing down the street. Then we went out for lunch, and it was a most miserable meal.

It seemed that the days when just to lunch out with Gilbert had been exciting, had vanished forever. Between us now was an unbridgeable gulf.

Soon after we returned to the flat, there came a ring at the door. I opened it to Hugh Maxwell.

'So you haven't flown yet,' he commented as he walked in. 'I was informed at your hotel that you had gone out, and I guessed where. Why has Milo got men trailing me, Brand?'

'Has he?' asked Gilbert.

'Yes. Most amusing. Still thinking of taking Kathryn away, Brand?'

'What the devil has it to do with you?'

'I'm not quite sure, but I warn you that bigamy is a serious offence. I could get you a good many months in prison on that count alone, but for blackmailing activities the spell would be years. I'd like that. Forget about persuading Kathryn to run away with you, or the police will learn that you committed deliberate bigamy twelve months ago.'

For a moment, I thought Gilbert was going to hurl himself at Hugh.

'Is that all you came here for?'

'More or less. And, of course, if Kathryn would like to return to her hotel, I'll see she arrives there.'

'I'm going back there tonight,' I said.

I thought I detected relief in Hugh Maxwell's eyes.

'You could go now,' he said.

'I — I — want to talk with Gilbert.'

'And now that your gallant offer is refused,' sneered Gilbert, 'you will find the door straight ahead.'

Hugh left the flat unperturbed. Gilbert watched from a window. His gaze was fixed narrowly on the distant pavement down the block. I joined him quietly. He was intently watching Hugh Maxwell climb into a private car.

'Some day I'll ask Milo to have him

rubbed out,' said Gilbert softly.

And for the next hour I knew his mind was full of the scheme, even while I tried desperately to make him talk, to convince him that crime was no good.

It was all so useless. The whole day passed while Gilbert smoked moodily, or sat at a bureau making notes and burning them. I lingered, hoping and trying to persuade him. Once Gilbert phoned Milo. He took care that little he said made any sense to me. We went out to dinner, still coldly polite, and it was after the meal, while we were watching a perfunctory cabaret show, that the little man known as Dave sidled up to our table. To my eyes, remembering his cheap suit and hat, he looked a little odd in evening dress.

'Milo wants you, Mr. Brand,' said Dave, and he spoke out of the corner of his mouth as if the restaurant was a prison workshop and the patrons suspicious warders. 'You and the girl,' he added.

Gilbert slowly stubbed out his cigarette. I saw his jaw muscles twitch.

'Why Kathryn? And where?'

'I dunno, Mr. Brand. Milo gave me the order. Definite, he said. I can tell you you've got to go with me to the Voodoo Club.'

'Voodoo Club! Don't tell me Milo has an interest in that!'

Dave smiled, but said nothing.

It was when we were on our way out, through the lounge, that I noticed Gilbert make an almost unnoticeable movement to shift the weight of something bulky from his overcoat pocket to his jacket.

I knew instinctively it was a revolver.

8

Milo's Machinations

The Voodoo Club, whatever that strange name might imply, was just a dark, drab building. Set in a crooked street in the heart of South London, the premises might have housed any activity.

After walking along badly-illuminated passages, we descended a flight of stairs to some cellars. Queer, I thought, how those who walk outside the law prefer cellars as a setting for their nefarious deeds.

Gilbert and I were guided into a dimly lighted room which somewhat resembled a meeting hall. Chairs and tables were arranged in a semi-circle. There was a sort of cabaret stage and, sitting in a recess of the poorly-lighted place, a small orchestra was playing some soft, weird music. A good many tables were occupied by men and women, and it seemed that the patrons of the club enjoyed the murky light. I could hear all around me a subdued murmur of conversation.

Then we were sitting before the diminutive stage. I noted its furnishings — a table and chair and a marble slab on wooden legs.

Gilbert sat beside me, his coat unbuttoned. I loosened my fur cape, feeling the stale air oppressive. Then a voice on my right said: 'Glad to see you're here, Mrs. Brand.'

Milo's husky voice.

I turned and saw his unmistakable bulk two seats from mine. Between us was the little thug known as Dave.

I longed to ask questions. Why had we been ordered to this strange club? I was sure that Gilbert and I were present for some set purpose. What was likely to happen? Apart from a feeling of tenseness, I was oddly unafraid. After all, Gilbert was by my side, and as to my surroundings, the place was simply a nondescript 'dive'.

But had I known what was to happen, I should have indeed trembled.

Gilbert gave me a cigarette, and as his lighter flared in the semi-gloom, the orchestra burst into a weird tune. People left the tables and began to dance to this odd, unfamiliar air.

A waiter sidled out of the gloom and placed drinks near to us on a long narrow table. I had not heard anyone place an order. I guessed Milo was influential in this strange Soho den, and had arranged everything previously.

I whispered to Gilbert: 'Why are we here?'

'Just sit still.' There was a wary note in his voice.

Milo had heard me whisper, for he said: 'What do you think of the Voodoo Club, my dear Kathryn?'

'I think it is smelly and stupid.'

He chuckled.

'It does not have its name for nothing,' he said, and he chuckled as at some hidden joke.

I would have danced with Gilbert just for the chance to talk, but the impossible music deterred me from asking him. I reached out for my glass, mostly from habit. The wine was sweet and cloying. I had never tasted it before. I replaced the glass and we all sat in silence, watching the dancers go through a pseudo-native dance with obvious pleasure.

'Can't we leave?' I asked Gilbert again. 'There seems little reason for us to be here.'

'Why has Kathryn to be here, Milo?' Gilbert ventured.

'Because it interests me,' was the calm reply. 'You can believe I want to study her reaction.'

Meaningless words, I thought. Was Milo slightly mad? I also realized the words conveyed an order. Whether we liked it or not, we could not leave. But why should Milo bring us to this place? I searched for the most obscure reasons and somehow the thought stuck in my mind that soon there might be more than a spectator's role for Gilbert and myself.

The music stopped and the dancers returned to their tables. Conversations drifted across the large cellar. Waiters were busy, moving dexterously in the gloom.

Suddenly the orchestra began to play a plaintive melody and at the same time a turbaned oriental in theatrical silk costume sprang on to the cabaret stage. He raised his hands and from some gloomy recess in the ceiling a body, covered by a sheet, lying stiff on a board was lowered to the marble slab.

I stared in wonder at this sudden bizarre act. What on earth was under the sheet? For a moment I felt inclined to laugh at such silly dramatics in a third-rate nightclub. Then the turbaned man advanced slowly. He was moving towards me!

I stiffened.

'Gilbert! Take me away!'

I heard Gilbert's chair scrape and then Milo's voice.

'Take it easy, Brand. It's nothing. I promise she won't be harmed.'

'What are you trying to do, Milo?' snapped Gilbert. 'I want to know your game.'

'You are taking orders from me,' said Milo, unpleasantly. 'I've said she won't be harmed.'

And Gilbert subsided to his seat. I felt better. I remembered the gun he carried. If he loved me, he should have used the gun to extricate me from this dreadful cellar. But Gilbert was afraid of Milo, and his fear was greater than his affection for me.

And then I was looking into two yellow eyes. The turbaned man brought his ugly face revoltingly close to mine. As I strained back, I could feel his heavy breathing, see the perspiration on his lined forehead. But above all else his eyes were like luminous orbs. They seemed to possess me as I stared back for a second or two.

Those seconds were my undoing. I realize now that I was being hypnotised. If only I had risen to my feet; tried to fight, the spell might not have fallen over me.

My last deliberate thought was how strange and crazy it was that all this should happen in a London cellar, with millions of ordinary decent folk about in the great city. But happen it did!

And then I felt suddenly calm. I could not think, but everything was pleasantly tranquil. I ceased to tremble, and I felt as though I was waiting for something. It is difficult to describe my exact feelings, but it seemed that I was ready to undertake some easy task or duty.

A knife was placed in my hand. I grasped it tightly, yet calmly. I stared straight ahead even when the perspiring hypnotist moved aside. Then I rose. Someone had given a command. I walked across the short clear space to the marble slab. I stopped before the white-sheeted body.

My arm slowly lifted while I stared down as if in a dream. I did not know what lay beneath the sheet, and I did not think about it.

The order floated to my brain. Strike! Strike!

My arm came flashing down. The knife struck with sickening force into the Thing.

I stood transfixed and released the knife. Blood had spurted up to my hand. A jeering laugh sounded behind me. A harsh exclamation from Gilbert, and then the crushing, compelling force within my brain rolled away.

Horror-stricken, I tried to wipe the blood from my hand. I heard an excited buzz of approval from the onlookers in the cellar. But I knew the blood was real.

Milo jumped forward and whipped the sheet from the shrouded body.

'Now my troublesome lady,' he jeered, 'you're a murderess and as bad as anyone else. You're one of us. Look who you've killed!'

Claudia lay under the sheet. An ugly red patch welled round a wound in her breast.

I fainted.

9

This is a Showdown

Something cool was stinging my face.

I opened my eyes. Gilbert was splashing water over my forehead. I was lying on a chair in a small room. The vastly better lighting told me that I was out of the Voodoo Club cellar. Then, like a nightmare, a vision of Claudia lying on the execution slab swept into my horrified mind.

I had been the executioner!

The grisly knowledge jerked my senses fully alert. I sat up, looked straight at Gilbert. Milo was close behind him, a callous smirk spreading across his pale face.

'I — I — didn't know what I was doing! I swear I didn't! It was a beastly scheme!' Then I suddenly calmed in an unaccountable manner. 'Gilbert, you've got to take me away from here.'

'Gilbert takes orders from me,' murmured Milo. 'The show is not yet over. Everyone stays.'

I clutched Gilbert's hand.

'Take me out of this awful place. Say you will, Gilbert!'

'I cannot!'

'But you can,' I said desperately.

Then Milo's husky voice: 'Glad you're seeing things my way, Gilbert.' Milo turned, spoke to me. 'Gilbert sticks by me because I can give him a certain profitable job in the near future. And you'll take my orders from now on, because if you don't I've plenty of witnesses who'll swear you killed Claudia and that you regularly visit the Voodoo Club.'

'But I did not know what I was doing!'

'That's a laugh,' jeered Milo. 'You kill a woman with a knife. You stab a dame to death and then say you didn't know why you did it.'

'But it is true!' I screamed.

'It's true you killed Claudia,' said Milo viciously. 'Don't ever forget that.'

'I was hypnotized! *You* knew she was

under that awful sheet. You wanted her dead! That was your revenge!'

'Bunk!' Milo went over to a door and opened it. 'Come on, Gilbert. As I said, the show is not yet over. There is something pretty interesting to follow. You'll like it, Gilbert.'

And then I felt sick at heart when Gilbert made the thinnest protest.

'Can't Kathryn stay here? Or go home? I swear she'll be no trouble.'

'No. This is a showdown. I'm fixing things so that there won't be any trouble from anyone, and that includes you, Kathryn, Claudia and' — Milo paused effectively — 'Maxwell.'

There was dead silence for an appreciable moment. Then Milo turned the door handle.

'You, Gilbert,' he said, 'will work much better in future if Kathryn is afraid to look at a cop or a private dick. Claudia crossed me, and she's paid. And Maxwell is too darned nosey. He's got to be disposed of. He's reached the stage where he can't keep out of my affairs.'

A few minutes later I was half-dragged

from the cellar-room back to the underground meeting place of the terrible Voodoo Club. My feelings were black and bitter when once again Gilbert made no protest at the treatment I was receiving.

But these thoughts were shocked from me when I looked up from my seat to see Hugh Maxwell led to the chair in the central space.

He was bleeding and his clothes were torn. He had been fighting, I knew. I cried out to him:

'Hugh. I'm here! Oh, Hugh, why did you let them get you?'

'Because I was too smart,' chuckled Milo's voice in the dark, devilish place. 'I had him watched — and then wham! My men just swooped. Here is Mr. Maxwell. He's a dick. Got so nosey, he signed his own death warrant.'

Hugh was peering through the gloom in my direction.

'Milo, send Kathryn away. You've got me. Send her away, and I'll be no trouble.'

'We don't mind a little trouble,' jeered Milo.

Hugh tried an appeal to Gilbert.

'Why don't you get her out of here? If you cared the slightest bit for her, Brand, you'd get her out of this filthy hole.'

'Keep your confounded mouth closed!' snarled Gilbert.

Two big evil-looking thugs caught Hugh's arms as he struggled. Then one produced a knife and held it within an inch of Hugh's throat. He calmed down and sat still in the chair.

Hugh tried again. 'Get her out of here, Brand!' he shouted. 'She loves you!'

It was then, in that evil place, that a startling revelation came to me, like a sudden ray of sunshine in the darkness. I knew that Hugh loved me, and that I loved him — inescapably, completely!

And I knew, too, that my love for Gilbert was dead, dead and gone for always. He had killed my love for him. I felt I did not care what happened to him now. His callousness, his crooked ideals and lack of scruples had beaten out the steady little flame of love that had lived in my heart. In that moment, to think of him, left only a cold, unresponsive feeling in me. There was no ache, no yearning now to reform him. Gilbert was dead to me. I did not want him ever to touch me again. Then I remembered the gun he carried in his pocket. The gun he could have used to save me from the horrible ordeal Milo had devised in order to kill Claudia and trap me.

If I could only get that gun, surely there would be a way out?

Slowly, one of the captors picked up some cord from the table, and advanced towards Hugh.

They were going to bind him. I knew I must act now or never!

Suddenly I put my arms round Gilbert, who was sitting next to me, just as he had on the first occasion.

'Oh, Gilbert darling, I'm afraid for you,' I nearly choked over the words, 'and I hate this place!'

'Aren't you afraid for Maxwell?' he lipped.

My arms moved erratically about him, as if I was approaching hysteria. I felt the bulk of the gun in his jacket pocket.

My hand slipped into the pocket while

I clung tightly to his neck with my other arm.

Then swiftly I leaped away. I had the heavy gun.

I do not know how I reached Hugh's side. I had leaped backwards from Gilbert, and then twisted desperately to face Hugh.

He had reacted like a man trained in dangerous ways. He had seen me scramble to him, and in the same second fought free from the two ruffians holding him. Everything was so rapid and I was so confused, I hardly knew what was happening. But as the thugs reached out to grasp Hugh again, I felt the gun wrenched from my hand.

'Stand back!'

Hugh's command arrested all further movement on the ruffians' part. I heard a click as the safety catch was pulled back on the revolver. Hugh thrust me behind him, and his gun pointed unwaveringly at Milo, Gilbert and Dave.

'Stay put, all of you!'

The warning was addressed to Milo and Gilbert in particular.

They had risen to pursue me. They froze at the threat of the gun. Hugh backed me along an aisle among the tables to a door. There was no sound as we retreated through the cellar, but as we reached the door, Milo jerked a low audible, 'Get him!'

Simultaneously he and Gilbert threw themselves to the ground among the scant shelter of chairs and tables.

At that moment, with incredible speed, a knife left the hand of one of the thugs who had held Hugh, and the blade came singing through the air as if powered by more than human force.

But Hugh had sensed the danger with that sixth sense which so fitted him for his work. He knocked me aside and fell to the floor after me.

The knife stabbed dully into the plaster wall above our heads.

Then I was deafened by the roar of the gun. In the cellar the sound was terrific. Twice Hugh fired. I glimpsed the knife-thrower twist fantastically as he fell to the ground.

Then, mingled with the echoes of the

second shot, I heard a choking cry of pain.

'Milo!' grated Hugh.

He rose, and sent another shot into the huddle of chairs and tables, as we darted into a passage.

Hugh was behind me in seconds, and kept that position while we turned from one passage to another. The place was an incredible warren, and I know now why the underworld prefers life in the cellars! We climbed a flight of stairs and burst into a room where half-a-dozen occupants at a card table scattered in sheer terror at Hugh's grim manner and the pointed gun. We went straight on down more crooked passages and through grimy apartments. Then we found ourselves in a hall leading to the street.

There were no pursuers. Hugh took my arm, impelled me down into the street and supported me. I had lost my fur cape and the cold night air struck at me, though it was a relief from the stifling atmosphere of that dreadful house behind us.

Hugh waved down a passing taxi, and

gave instructions to the driver that I did not hear. Then he turned and bundled me into the taxi. As we moved off, he turned to me

'Milo taunted me when I was trussed up in another room. Said he was going to have me killed slowly as so many have died in the Voodoo Club. He also said you'd killed Claudia.'

And then I poured out the ghastly story to him.

'You needn't worry, Kathryn,' he said at last, taking my hand. 'It was a frame-up. Claudia was dead when she was laid on that slab. Milo is a sadist if ever there was one. When Claudia's body was brought back from the stage Milo showed me the wound in her body. But I also noticed a bullet wound in her head.'

'Surely Gilbert would have guessed that,' I exclaimed. 'He never tried to help me.'

'His wits are keen enough for most things,' was Hugh's reply, 'and I'll bet he knew it was a frame-up.'

'Where are we going?' I asked.

'To the nearest police station,' Hugh said.

* ★ ★

The following weeks were an anxious time for me — and for Hugh. To my consternation, on reaching the police station, Hugh had handed over the gun and told the police he had had to shoot his way out of the Voodoo Club. He would make a full statement, but in the meantime he urged the police to raid the place immediately, where they would find the murdered body of Claudia — Jean Metcalfe — and the men responsible.

Whilst we were held in custody the police did so, and whilst most of the people had fled — including Gilbert — they found the dead body of Claudia — and also Milo. He had been shot by Hugh as we had fought our way clear. Things might have been awkward for Hugh, despite my testimony that he had only fired in self defence, but fortunately for us, the police found the thug who had thrown the knife. They also found the knife with the thug's fingerprints on it, still embedded in the plaster wall. The thug had only been wounded by Hugh's shot, and he had been left for dead, lying unconscious beside Milo's body, whilst the rats in the Voodoo Club — Gilbert amongst them — had scattered. When he recovered sufficiently he was questioned by the police, and he made a full confession. His statement accorded with Hugh's and my own, and he was also able to testify that Milo had shot Claudia before the ghastly hypnotic episode involving me. Further, he was able to give the identities of several members of the gang — including the hypnotist himself — and the police were able to find most of them and make arrests. But Gilbert had managed to escape.

I am trying now to forget Gilbert and everything about him — even the best things, for while he did love me at one time, he did not love me sufficiently to give up crime and the double life he led. I think Gilbert may have left the country and gone to America, even as he had once planned, but he is now a fugitive, and the police will eventually find him.

Thus Milo's racket was broken, for, I think, he alone possessed the necessary information to continue the blackmailing activities.

Denis Selby was another victim of the tragic sequence of events, but time would heal his hurts. His testimony, too, served to clear Hugh from any possible charges.

After the police investigation was over, I moved into a smaller flat, and tried to live on my small allowance from my guardian in the Midlands. I discovered that simple pleasures were just as enjoyable as a mad whirl of spending. It dawned on me that Gilbert might have spoiled me forever if events had not turned out as they had.

Strangely enough Hugh never pressed me to marry him until one day I visited his office. We were alone in the little room with its leather settees and desk.

'What is it, Hugh?' I asked him point-blank.

He looked uncomfortable and said, 'What do you mean Kathryn?'

'I won't say you're avoiding me, but you're so strangely silent and — and — impersonal when we meet. What is it Hugh?'

And then it came out.

'You still love Gilbert Brand, don't you, Kathryn?' There was a deep burning gleam in his fine eyes. 'You got that gun from him, but I heard you call him 'darling'. Well, Kathryn, I happen to love you, but I don't want to say anything if you're not interested.'

I was very close to him. I've never seen a man look so uncomfortable; I wanted to kiss him, and I did, suddenly and softly on the lips.

His rugged features are not classical, but he has marvellous eyes. They gleam and show his whole nature like a mirror.

'I don't love Gilbert. I never want to see him again; and I doubt if I shall. I think I'm going to completely forget him. It is the only thing to do,' I said.

'What a dope I am!' He put his arms around me. He kissed me long and — well, most people know what it is like to be kissed!

'Of course, I always knew I'd marry you,' he said apologetically. 'Will you marry me?'

'Oh, you idiot, of course! We'll be so

happy,' I said. 'I love you, Hugh. That's what I called to see you about!'

He took me in his arms.

And this is the last time I'll write or think of Gilbert Brand.

2

BLACK BROW

1

At Greer House

Christine Ashton glanced across the carriage at the young man in brown tweeds. She was glad that the train was nearing Kirkdale, a Westmorland village. Three hours ago the young man had spoken about the pleasant weather, and she had checked her ready smile and murmured something formal.

She had remembered her uncle's peculiar warning. He had asked her not to mention her destination to anyone and to avoid talking to any stranger.

Christine found a cold attitude difficult to maintain. For one thing her lips broke into a smile far too easily. Her grey eyes danced at the slightest excuse. She knew she was apt to get excited about the most ordinary happenings, such as a new hat, a dance ticket, a new baby — oh, anything!

So at least she could have spoken to the

young man in brown tweeds but for her uncle's grim warning.

Stephen Meldrum was a grim man. He was moody and resentful at being struck off the Medical Association Roll for shady practices when at the height of his skill as a doctor.

Christine owed a debt to Stephen Meldrum. For when she was a child his skill had saved her from dying during an attack of pneumonia. So Christine had complied with her uncle's request that she spend her month's holiday at Greer House.

Christine supposed her attitude of rebuff was ridiculous, but Stephen Meldrum had been emphatic. In his depressing letters he had asked her to promise not to join in conversation with any stranger while she was travelling, and this was important if the stranger was a man.

Kirkdale. The train was slowing for the station. She reached for her case on the rack, and the young man rose with remarkable speed and hauled it down for her.

'Been a pleasant trip,' he said smilingly. Then his strong white teeth clamped on this pipe stem again as he turned to reach for his own bag.

So he was getting off at Kirkdale! In that case, they would probably be the only passengers to descend, for few people called at the silent village during weekdays.

Would Stephen think that odd or sinister?

Christine lost sight of the young man in the train corridor, and when she passed the ticket collector and saw Stephen Meldrum waiting for her, the young man was not in sight.

'Well, I've arrived, uncle.'

'The train is late,' he said bitterly.

Years ago she had known him as a neat professional man. Actually she had seen him twice in the past six years and the last occasion was exactly a year ago.

'Your bags will be sent up to Greer House, I suppose?'

'Yes, I have one case with me,' she replied.

She had travelled many miles to meet Stephen Meldrum, and she ached to ask him why he had asked her so earnestly to come to Greer House and why he was afraid that people might learn of her destination. She wanted to learn more about Greer House — what an odd name!

She would set the ball rolling soon, she decided.

At that particular moment the young man in brown tweeds was staring through the dirty pane of the diminutive waiting room. His eyes were fixed thoughtfully on the girl's face. She could not see him, he knew, for the room was dingy and outside the sun was shining. His grasp of such matters was always instinctive, for which ability he had many times in his life been grateful.

A minute later he left the waiting room, for the new car had driven away.

Christine felt she must ask about Greer House.

'Do you like living there, uncle?'

'I would hardly live there if I did not like it, Christine. It has many attractions. I am able to do a bit of fishing in the stream that falls from Black Brow. I have the run of the house and grounds and it

— er — suits me. Adam Barlow and his wife Emily look after Greer House. Adam is gamekeeper and general guardian of Black Brow, and his wife looks after me.'

'Black Brow!' repeated Christine. 'That is an odd name!'

'It is the name of a hill. The locals in Kirkdale call the rising ground above Greer House the Black Brow because in the gloaming the thick pines give the crest a dark appearance — like a black brow.'

'Heavens! Will I like it? I hope it is not haunted.'

'Of course the villagers have their stories about the place. That is why they give it such a ridiculous name. They will not venture near the hill anywhere near gloaming, and I am glad for I hate people wandering round the place. They spoil my fishing. There is a waterfall near the top of Black Brow, then the stream flows placidly and passes Greer House.'

'Oh.' She felt rather blank. 'How much longer do you think you'll have to care for Greer House?'

'I've been guardian of Greer House and its grounds for just ten months,' he said slowly. He changed to low gear for a stiff gradient. 'I carry on my task until the owner returns. Yes, until Simon Blacknall returns. That was the instruction I received when my employer went abroad. No matter how long he is away, I have to keep Greer House in working order for his return.'

'Do you hear often from him?'

'Yes, yes. Quite often,' he said curtly.

'I'm glad you have such a pleasant job,' she said warmly. 'The owner of Greer House must be a generous man.'

'Simon Blacknall generous!' he sneered. 'He is wicked. He is wickedness personified! Do not speak his name inside Greer House. Never, never,' said Stephen vehemently, 'speak the name Simon Blacknall in Greer House.

'As I say, Simon Blacknall was an inhuman monster,' continued her uncle. 'He is still alive, of course, but I don't know where. He is a big man — a giant! There is animal cruelty in his face and venom in his voice.'

She stammered: 'Oh!'

'You did not tell anyone about your

destination?' he asked suddenly.

'Oh, no. I was very careful. But why had I not to mention the fact?'

'I have enemies,' he said testily.

'Why did you send for me?' she asked.

The question made him more irritated. His eyes screwed up, and his lips tightened.

The flinty road wound over barren hedgeless country, and the car swayed at high speed. Yet Stephen Meldrum handled the car like an expert.

Christine clung to a handle and asked again:

'Why did you send for me, uncle?'

'The truth is I need a friend. You are the only person I really know and can trust. I must have a friend — I must. I have told you I have enemies. I hope you will help me, and obey me implicitly, even though you do not understand.'

'I'll help you,' she said. 'But are you sure you are not ill — ?'

'I am not ill!' he snapped.

They approached Greer House suddenly. It lay behind a long stone wall which was crumbling in places. A drive led to the house, which was set among pines and wild foliage. The edifice was a mixture of different architectural periods. Over a hundred years there had been alterations and additions.

After garaging the car in the old stables, they entered the house. Stephen went immediately to his study and she followed. He took down a small jar and extracted two pellets. He swallowed them quickly.

'I'll show you to your room,' he said. He turned to a gong that lay beside a black oak hallstand. He rapped the brass gently with a leather-tipped stick.

Emily Barlow appeared a few minutes later. She came down a staircase at the far end of the passage. Christine saw a heavy, plain-faced woman in a scrupulously white apron. Her jet-black hair was parted severely in the centre. She wore a dark dress under the apron, and the sleeves were tightly buttoned to the wrists.

'So you are Christine Ashton,' she commented.

'Everything is ready for my niece?' he inquired.

'Has been for two days,' said Emily Barlow dryly.

The housekeeper strode on, and to the girl it seemed the woman had a masterful tread. Presently, after climbing a creaking staircase, they came to the room chosen for Christine.

It was quite nice, she had to admit.

'But everything looks new,' she exclaimed.

'I bought it for you, Christine,' he said, and gave a twisted smile. 'I want you to enjoy your stay here.'

'You've seen the room,' the house-keeper said. 'Come along. We'll show you the rest of the house that you can use.'

'That is very important, Christine,' smiled Stephen Meldrum. 'You see, we actually use very little of the house. The entire top floor is never entered.'

'Don't they collect a lot of dust?' asked Christine innocently.

'Perhaps. But my orders are that those rooms are not to be opened.'

'Then they are locked?'

'Yes. I hope you will promise not to wander upstairs. You must never go near them.'

'Why?'

'Please, Christine! There are certain

orders which must be obeyed without question, because this is not my house.'

'Well, I wonder if I could see Black Brow?'

'It isn't very interesting,' interposed Emily Barlow. 'Still, you can see the hill from the conservatory at the back of the house. Come along.'

Faintly, Christine was beginning to dislike that commanding 'come along'.

Then from the conservatory, she saw someone moving across the open ground immediately behind the house. It was a man and he was small and bent. He carried a sack and his clothes seemed so dirty they resembled the sack in texture.

'That is Adam Barlow,' said Stephen calmly.

That work-stained labourer Emily's husband! Christine stole a glance at the woman's face and she saw the house-keeper bite her lower lip.

Strangely at that moment some sixth sense must have made the man on the ground stare up at the people watching him. For an appreciable time he stood, his mouth open, his sack on the ground, his hands dangling by his side. Then he broke into a cackle that Christine could hear even through the glass conservatory. Adam Barlow swung up his sack, and laughing like one possessed, slouched off.

'Adam Barlow is mad, Christine,' said Stephen. 'Completely mad.'

2

Enter Claud

Christine raised confused eyes to Emily Barlow.

'I am so sorry,' she said.

'Do not think about him,' she said calmly.

There was a clatter of a horse and cart in the drive. It was Christine's luggage sent up from the station. She seized on the cases and had them brought up to her bedroom. Once in the modern room she seemed apart from the rest of the depressing house, and her spirits rose. She changed out from her tailored costume and put on a frock of simply cut blue linen.

A few minutes later Mrs. Barlow brought her some tea and buttered crumpets. Christine suddenly realized how hungry she was.

The sun was still going strong some

twenty minutes later, and she slipped on a teddy bear coat over her dress and ran downstairs and let herself out on to the drive. She did not meet Stephen or Mrs. Barlow and light-heartedly she stepped out.

She came to the road and decided to roam down the wall that bordered Greer House and its grounds. She stepped over the rough turf — a delightful figure with her dark, shining hair waving in the light wind.

All at once she came across the little cottage nesting in the hollow. At the front of its careless garden ran the stream that came down from Black Brow and wound its way past Greer House. The small cottage hugged the banks that enclosed it so tightly, that it was not surprising she had run into it so unexpectedly.

A lanky man looked up from his sprawling position on the cottage's few feet of lawn.

'I say, who are you?' he asked immediately.

'Who are you?' retorted Christine, laughing.

'Oh, I'm Claud Arnell. Accent on the last syllable, if you please! I live here — quite alone, you know. I adore it. I've been looking at the stream all the afternoon.

'Is that all you have to do?' she asked impishly.

'I'm a poet,' protested the young man. 'Looking at the water gave me a marvellous line. Are you staying here?'

'I'm staying at Greer House with my uncle.'

His foolish chin seemed to drop in astonishment.

'Good heavens! I don't know how you dare!' His hand went to his mouth in an affected manner. 'I know a great many things about Greer House,' he said confidingly.

'Oh, do you?'

'If I were you I'd go away immediately. It is not safe to stay at Greer House.'

'What do you mean?'

'My dear girl, Stephen Meldrum is mad. In fact, they're all mad.'

'My uncle is not mad! How dare you say so!'

'Everyone in the village knows they're mad. They're waiting for Simon Blacknall when the man has been dead two years. Everyone in Kirkdale knows about him. He's been dead as mutton for two years, my dear.'

'Simon Blacknall is not dead,' said Christine confidently. 'My uncle told me he is abroad. I believe him.'

'That's funny. Three people from the village saw him fall to his death from the rocks round the waterfall on Black Brow. That was two years ago.'

'I don't believe it.'

'Well!' he gasped. 'You should know the truth, by jove. I really think it is up to me to protect you. I'll take you to the three people in Kirkdale who will tell you how Simon Blacknall met his death. They were all working for the man at the time.'

'How do you know all this?' she demanded. 'Is it true?'

'Certainly. Three people can show you Simon Blacknall's grave. He was buried in the centre of Black Brow. Several villagers were present. They acted as pallbearers. Jolly tough ground, you know, to haul such a big brute over.'

Christine hesitated.

'Shall I take you down to the village?' asked Claud Arnell eagerly. 'I happen to have two bikes.'

'I could hardly ride a gentleman's machine.'

'Oh, but one has an open frame,' he said.

Because she was greatly troubled, she assented. They cycled down the hilly road into Kirkdale. Claud Arnell babbled about his poetry and wobbled dangerously at the same time. But they arrived at a little general dealer's shop in Kirkdale's main street.

'Mr. Wardle, this is — ' Claud Arnell stopped.

'My name is Christine Ashton.'

'Nice name. Sam, Miss Ashton is staying at Greer House, and she would like to hear about Simon Blacknall. Didn't you bury him, Sam?'

'Ay, young man, I helped to. Jim Prudhoe and Billy Baines and me.'

'Who saw him fall into the waterfall?'

'Jim Prudhoe, man. I've told ye before.'

'I know, I know. Now tell Christine — I — er — mean, Miss Ashton, who the other people were who were present.'

'They were Adam Barlow and his wife.'

'Emily Barlow and Adam!' repeated Christine.

'No, Miss,' said Sam Wardle kindly. 'Old Adam was not married to that woman at that time. He were married to his first wife. Liz. They were birds of a feather, don't you see, but she died shortly after Simon were buried. Then Emily married Adam.'

'She married him only two years ago!' gasped Christine.

'Ay. She came to the house just after Simon's death. In fact the day he was buried. Nobody had ever seen her before. Then old Liz died, and before you could say fell dykes Emily had married Adam.'

'I don't know what to say — but — thank you!'

'Now do you believe me?' Claud Arnell was completely blind to the girl's white, troubled face.

'I shall go to my uncle and ask him to explain,' said the girl steadily.

They mounted the bikes and rolled away down the street. Once more she had to listen to this incredibly superficial young man's conversation. At last they came to his cottage where Christine jumped off her machine and prepared to hand it over to its owner.

'The cheeky blighter!' Christine heard him gasp.

'What's wrong?' she called out.

'Fellow in my cottage!' he replied indignantly; and then to someone below in his gardens, he said: 'I say, you! You can't do that, you know. Walk all over my place. I suppose I left the door unlocked.'

'You certainly did, Claud,' said a pleasant voice.

'I say,' said Claud Arnell, aggrieved. 'How did you know my name is Claud?'

'Coincidence, old chap. I call everyone Claud!'

3

The Name Is Melvyn Trent

'Nice place you have here,' said the young man in brown tweeds.

'Yes, isn't it? I — ' Claud Arnell stopped and scowled.

'The truth is,' admitted the young man, 'I wandered along the bank of the stream, and I suddenly felt thirsty. I knocked on your door, saw it was open and thought I heard someone say 'Come in'.'

'Oh, indeed. Who are you?' asked Claud Arnell peevishly.

The poet seemed to have a lot of curiosity about people, thought Christine.

'The name is Melvyn Trent,' said the young man slowly. 'Ever heard of it?'

'Of course not. Why should I?'

Melvyn Trent did not reply, but glanced at the girl.

Christine took to introducing herself, seeing that Claud Arnell had not thought

147

about it. Why not? She was certainly curious about Melvyn Trent.

'I'm Christine Ashton. I'm staying at Greer House.'

He did not inform her that was a point he already knew.

With a glare that was merely comical, Claud Arnell passed the other man. The poet went up to his cottage and closed the door.

Turning, he found Christine and Melvyn Trent staring at the stream at the bottom of his garden. He rejoined them.

Melvyn Trent found much of interest in the rainbow-coloured film that swirled slowly past. The coloured swirl was thin and light, but he knew it was oil.

'May I ask if you are on holiday, Miss Ashton?' remarked Melvyn, turning to the girl.

'Yes, I am staying a month with my uncle.'

'I'm on holiday, too. Staying a month at the Blacksmith's Arms in Kirkdale. Your uncle's house has a strange name and the name of the pine forest behind is quite menacing. And the tales I heard in the

Blacksmith's Arms are quite alarming.'

'What did you hear?' she asked directly.

'Well, it wasn't the usual haunted house stuff, but they as good as hinted that everyone in Greer House is mad because they are waiting for a dead man.'

'Well, I — I — my uncle is taking care of the house until his employer returns.' said Christine in her bewilderment. 'I'm sure my uncle isn't mad, though he is a little strange. If Simon Blacknall is dead, I — I — don't understand how my uncle can be staying on at Greer House.'

'No. Queer, isn't it?' murmured Melvyn Trent. 'You haven't seen your uncle for a long time until today?'

'The last time I saw him was twelve months ago. He has changed in some ways. Once he was neat and efficient. Now he is drab and I think he is ill.'

'In which way is he ill?'

'He is acting strangely.' She went on to tell him about part of the house being forbidden to her.

She had enjoyed getting her little perplexities off her mind. Her grey eyes began to look animated again. Melvyn

Trent saw a devilishly pretty girl before him, and his interest became suddenly a highly personal one.

'Whereabouts are the rooms which you haven't to go near?'

'On the top floor,' she told him.

'And you are here simply for a holiday?'

'Of course. In a way, I shall look after my uncle. He — he — said he needed a friend — someone he could trust.'

'Mrs. Barlow has cared for him for some time now, hasn't she? Do you think they have quarrelled?'

'I don't think so. And I don't want to talk about it any more,' she said curtly.

'Well, judging from the facts you've given me, I think you should look after your uncle. I think he needs someone like you.'

'Thank you. Perhaps you're right.'

'I am always right,' he said modestly, then added quickly: 'I say, Miss Ashton, if you're going back to Greer House, I'd be jolly glad to accompany you.'

'Yes, I should be going back.'

'I am going along the road,' said Melvyn, 'and naturally I'll see you along.

You should stay and lock your door, Claud.'

'Don't call me Claud!'

'I call lots of blokes Claud!' was the reply.

Melvyn Trent helped Christine across the rough turf, and Claud Arnell disappeared into his cottage. He stared at his mirror and what he saw was evidently annoying, for he kicked a stool as he turned, disgruntled.

Melvyn Trent and Christine approached the drive leading to Greer House and they halted.

'There you are,' he said. He looked interestedly at the old house. 'Which is your room?'

She indicated a window. She recognised it quickly by the gay curtains.

'Claud Arnell's cottage is very convenient,' he said abruptly. Then at a tangent: 'I suppose the other windows belong to secret rooms. They are certainly dingy. Almost impossible to see through them, I should think.'

'Why should the house have secret rooms?' she demanded. 'I think you are trying to frighten me!'

'I wonder what Black Brow looks like just at the moment?' remarked Melvyn Trent suddenly. 'Would you care to see it? We'll have to go round to the back of the house for a proper view.'

'How dark it is!' exclaimed Christine. Her tone was not enthusiastic. 'Let's go round to the front — it is much pleasanter!'

The next moment she froze at the sound of a man's voice.

'Simon Blacknall! Simon Blacknall!'

It was Adam Barlow. Stephen Meldrum stood beside him.

They were both oblivious to Melvyn and Christine.

'Simon Blacknall. Simon — '

'You fool!' shouted Stephen Meldrum. He hit the crazy old man. 'I'll kill you! Go to your room and stay there! Don't come out until morning! You understand?'

'I haven't fed Simon,' moaned Adam Barlow.

'Damn you! Be silent!'

They disappeared into the house, Stephen pushing and scuffling with the madman. Melvyn Trent looked gravely into Christine's eyes.

'You need help,' he said. 'But you'll be all right for the present. If I'm wrong, promise me you'll hang a light out from your room window.'

'Who — who — are you?'

A deep furrow appeared between his eyes. He looked at the ground.

'I may tell you tomorrow. You might dislike me someday. Stephen Meldrum is not a fool, you know,' he added mysteriously.

He led her round to the front entrance.

'Go inside, and do not tell your uncle whom you have met.'

'I shall lock my room door,' said Christine uneasily.

'A good idea.'

'Where are you going?' she asked.

'To Claud Arnell's cottage,' he said, and smiling he walked down the drive, stopping only once to wave encouragingly.

4

Noises in the Night

Mrs. Barlow was sitting at the table, and the girl noticed places were set for three.

'Your uncle began to wonder where you had gone.'

'I've been for a walk,' said Christine.

'Where to?'

'Oh, down by the river. I met an idiotic young man by the name of Claud Arnell.'

'I see. You met someone of your own age. I know him. He has been living there a month. To my mind he is a foolish idler.'

Suddenly her uncle came in, and Christine turned to him.

'So you have found your way back, Christine! I thought you had run away!' he joked pathetically.

'I've been out walking. I met a young man called Claud Arnell, and though he is extremely silly, I stopped to talk to him.'

'What did he tell you?' His voice trembled.

She plunged at the heart of her perplexities.

'He told me that your — your — employer' — she knew she had just evaded saying Simon Blacknall — 'is dead. That he had been buried on Black Brow. A man called Jim Prudhoe saw him fall into the rocky waterfall.'

'Christine, you must not ask why I keep this house open,' muttered Stephen Meldrum.

'You need not stay, Christine,' Mrs. Barlow said gently.

Stephen wheeled, his twisted lips furious.

'But she will stay. She is staying for a month.' He turned to the girl. 'You will stay, Christine? Promise me.'

'I'll stay,' said Christine steadily. 'But is your employer dead or alive?'

'He is dead,' mumbled Stephen Meldrum. 'If you must know, I suppose you could say he is dead.'

'Then you are keeping Greer House for a dead man?'

'You must not ask me questions,' he muttered.

Christine tackled her supper, and after

a while the fire died to red embers.

'We go to bed early,' said Mrs. Barlow.

'I'll take you up,' offered her uncle.

She was glad of his company as they traversed the dark passages. She knew she would feel afraid to move about alone in this big gloomy mansion.

He left her installed in her room. He returned to where Emily Barlow sat staring into the fire.

'You may make your niece very unhappy,' she said calmly.

'I need the company of a friend. My niece and I have a lot in common,' he said sweepingly.

'So you told me, but I can see that you are lying. You told me you had sent for your niece because she is very dear to you, and now I see how much you exaggerate. I knew it was not wise to have her here, but you seemed very eager.'

'I tell you, she is like a tonic to me,' he insisted.

'And if He meets her?' hinted the woman.

'That shouldn't happen if we are careful.'

'You know as well as I do there is always the possibility,' mocked the house-keeper.

Without a word he strode away and went to his study. There he donned a white coat and rubber gloves. As he moved round he muttered:

'She is mad. But she'll not take me with her to her certain end. Mad, foolish woman!'

He went out. He traversed the passages and at Adam Barlow's room paused to listen to a series of moans. Then, after a definite hesitation, he placed a key in a lock and went inside.

Christine had had her luxurious spell by the electric fire, and then she switched off and climbed into the rosewood bed.

She was completely unaware that the door handle turned as someone tried the door.

The horrifying moan that echoed through Greer House woke her instantly. She sat up, staring into the darkness, her heart thudding. She thought she had been asleep only a few minutes.

But terror stifled her thought. The

agonised moan fanned out again like the cry of a trapped monster. It subsided with a rumble.

She heard a man shout 'Emily!' and knew it was Stephen Meldrum. There came three resounding thuds and a rattle as though bars were being shaken. She heard the sound of running feet, and she got out of bed, her whole body trembling with the suddenness of it all.

Her feet touched the ground and she tried to stand. There did not seem sufficient strength in her limbs. She collapsed and as she fell she fainted. Greer House was silent.

5

Visit to Kirkdale

Within a second Christine realized she was lying on her bed. Mrs. Barlow had evidently picked her up and placed her there.

'Mrs. Barlow — what has happened?'

'It is nothing. Adam has had one of his spasms, that is all.'

'Then that ghastly moan was Adam?'

'It was Adam,' repeated the woman. 'He is quiet now.'

When she had left, Christine sat before the electric fire. It was a long time before she felt composed enough to think about sleep. When she did, she went to the door to turn the key. It was then it occurred to her that Emily Barlow was undoubtedly in possession of a duplicate key.

Perhaps the housekeeper had decided to visit the bedroom in order to explain the alarming sounds, and had found the door locked.

Over an excellent breakfast she said to Stephen Meldrum, 'Has Adam got over his attack?'

'Oh, yes. I'm so sorry you were frightened. You'll like this place after a while. Could I take you into Kirkdale?'

'When do you intend to go?'

'Immediately. I have to be back by midday. I have some work to do. You'll come, won't you, Christine?'

He seemed eager to convince her, and he added:

'I do not want to leave you alone with Emily Barlow. Perhaps I should not mention it, but I think she dislikes you.'

'Heavens! What have I done?'

'It isn't your fault. The loneliness here has affected her.'

'Why should she marry a madman?' asked Christine steadily.

'Emily has reasons of her own for marrying Adam Barlow,' said Stephen hurriedly.

'Aren't you aware of the reason?'

'It would upset you to hear them,' he said carefully.

'She, too, must be mad,' declared Christine sweepingly.

'Mrs. Barlow has been up all night,' said her uncle. 'She is still asleep.'

After breakfast she joined him in the expensive car. He drove down the drive and on to the road leading to Kirkdale.

Presently Stephen's spirits rose.

'You are working in London, aren't you? I should like to visit the city again.'

'Was Simon Blacknall very wealthy?' asked the girl suddenly.

'Well — yes. He was clever,' he said rapidly.

They entered the village, made one or two purchases. Stephen showed her the architectural oddities, and then glanced at his watch. 'We must be getting back.'

It was a surprise to Christine. They had been in the village barely three-quarters of an hour. She had thought her uncle's intention was to stay longer. She did not demur.

They climbed into the car and set off. Stephen was silent.

He began to hum an old tune in an effort to appear nonchalant. It was an incongruous experience. Christine kept a straight face after her first twitch of amusement.

'I'm forty-nine,' he said unexpectedly. 'Not very old. Could do many things yet. Could — um — start again.'

'You're still a youngish man,' she encouraged.

'Yes. Look, someone has had a breakdown,' he said, changing the subject. He pointed along the road at a car drawn up beside the ditch. He slowed his new car abreast of the stationary vehicle.

'We motorists must help one another,' he said good-humouredly.

She had not imagined him as a Good Samaritan. As he alighted, she made a move to follow him, but he held up a deterring hand.

'No need for you to bother, Christine. I'll not be long. The man may need only a spanner. I'll get my box from the rear locker.'

He disappeared, leaving her fully aware that his last few words had been in the nature of an order.

She sat patiently for a minute, and then turned to look through the small rear window, but a curtain had been drawn across the view. She wondered when the curtain had been drawn.

A minute later a shadow fell across the side window and as she glanced up the door was wrenched open and Stephen jumped in. At the same time Christine was aware that a man had tumbled into the rear seat and was gasping and cursing.

Stephen let the car forward with a sudden jerk, and the vehicle accelerated down the road, the engine roaring into a deep furious note. As he changed gear like an expert racing motorist, she looked at him in amazement.

Every line was puckered in concentrated anger. He sat tensed over the wheel. Christine turned to look at the man in the back seat. She saw an individual to whom she took an instant dislike. The man was a sallow faced person with a moustache. His forehead was narrow and his lips thin. His eyes held a nasty glint as they briefly met hers.

She swivelled to Stephen Meldrum.

'Why are you racing away?'

'Be quiet. I will explain later,' he jerked.

She sat back, mystified.

6

Mrs. Blacknall

'You're a bit of an idiot, aren't you, Claud?' remarked Melvyn Trent pleasantly, as he stared at the disappearing car containing Stephen Meldrum and the others.

'I couldn't help tripping,' said Claud, aggrieved. 'I think I fell over your beastly feet, anyway.'

'Well, we can meet Sid Manning at Greer House, if we hurry along on the bikes you have so kindly provided. Sid is a con-man and general trickster. When I saw him in Kirkdale, I knew there was only one possible reason for him being in this remote village.'

'What did you expect to find Meldrum up to?' inquired Claud.

'Well, when we trailed Manning to this spot and saw him stage his fake breakdown, I guessed he was preparing to meet

Meldrum. Now Stephen Meldrum makes one of his infrequent trips to the village and ever so accidentally meets Manning. There is only one conclusion. Meldrum was handing a new consignment of notes to Manning. Now I'd like to pin that on Sid Manning. Though Meldrum is the chap I'm after. If we'd started a mix-up like we intended, I might have been able to dive a hand inside Manning's pockets. However, let's get cracking, or your father will send me a strong note referring to the lack of results.'

'You know, I can't understand why Dad sent you along,' stated Claud. 'Dash it, he knew I had taken this job on in a purely voluntary spirit. Then he has the nerve to send you, a special investigator, and I find you snooping round my cottage. A rotten thing to do to a fellow. Dad might have told me all about you, at least.'

'I think Sir Bernard is anxious for quick results,' said Melvyn Trent soothingly. 'After all, these dud notes are causing his bank a great deal of trouble.'

He walked to the ditch and hauled his bike onto the road. Claud followed, an aggrieved expression still twisting his face.

'I can't get the hang of this. Who the dickens is making the dud money? After all, Simon Blacknall has been dead two years. Do you think Meldrum is printing the stuff?'

'He couldn't,' said Melvyn Trent briefly. 'Get on your machine.'

They began to cycle quickly down the road towards Greer House.

'Well, what about Mrs. Barlow?' puffed Claud.

'The notes are the work of the only man who could forge such pretty pictures,' said Melvyn carefully, 'and that man is Simon Blacknall. Your father would tell you that Blacknall was a master forger, and we were just getting a line on him when he was reported dead. The dud notes did not appear again for nearly twelve months after his death, and in the meantime we had collected most of the earlier stuff. Now forgeries which are undoubtedly the work of Simon Blacknall are being changed into real money all over the damned country.'

'But the man is dead! Everyone knows that!'

'Who says so?'

'Why — everyone — the coroner — everyone!' spluttered Claud. 'You can't fool doctors and coroners, old boy. The man is as dead as mutton.'

'Okay, Claud Arnell — what a poetic name! Much better than Claud Tippington. Does Sir Bernard approve of you dispensing with the family name?'

'My dear chap, I had to have another name when I rented the cottage,' snapped Claud Tippington. 'I couldn't snoop around when everyone knows about Tippington, the bankers.'

Melvvn Trent pounded at the pedals and presently the wall surrounding Greer House came into view. The two men dismounted from their machines and left them propped against the wall.

'Perhaps it would be a good idea to call and inform Sid Manning that his car is still lying at the roadside,' remarked Melvyn Trent. 'In any case, Meldrum will have the wind up now and be on the watch for us. To fix this case we've got to catch someone red-handed printing those notes.'

'Do you mean Simon Blacknall?' laughed Claud Tippington.

'I mean anyone. Have you noticed the oil that runs down the stream? There are frequent patches. An odd thing to notice in a stream flowing from a hilly waterfall don't you think?'

But Claud seemed incapable of grasping the point.

Even as they approached Greer House Stephen Meldrum's car swerved violently from the drive on to the road and without a second's pause, drove violently down the road and disappeared.

'We seem to be a bit late,' commented Melvyn, and he halted to fill his pipe. 'Manning was in that car.' He puffed steadily at his pipe. 'Obviously on his way back to London or Liverpool or maybe Glasgow. Who knows. Meldrum with him, too. But he'll be back soon, I guess. Now there's a phone in Greer House.'

He led the way up to the squat mansion. On the lawn he met Christine Ashton. She had been watching the departure of

Meldrum and his unknown passenger.

'Hello,' said Melvyn. 'So you slept well? At any rate you did not hang out a light.'

She stared at the two of them. How was it they were now so friendly?

'I wonder if your uncle would mind me using his phone?' asked Melvyn coolly.

'I — er — I — think you can use it. Anyway, he has just gone out in the car, so he is not here to object,' retorted Christine.

Melvyn went into Stephen Meldrum's room, where the phone was situated. After a short while he came out and joined Claud and Christine in the hall and simultaneously Emily Barlow came down a passage. She came slowly up to them, her dark clothes giving her an appearance of severity.

'Who are you?' she asked. Her eyes sought Melvyn's. 'Why are you here?'

He pressed down his pipe and wiped the ash from his finger before replying.

'Good morning, Mrs. Blacknall.'

She stood quite still. Melvyn brought out a small photograph. There was typewriting on the back, but his hand covered that. It seemed suspiciously like a police photograph.

'I should say, Mrs. Barlow,' corrected Melvyn Trent. 'Or should I?'

'You will please get out of here,' she retorted harshly.

'Of course.' He looked at the photograph again and then at the woman. 'Yes, Mrs. Blacknall. Strange world, isn't it?'

She was still watching them as they walked to the drive.

On an impulse, Christine ran to them. She walked a few yards with them.

'Please tell me what this is all about?'

'You're in the enemy camp,' Melvyn said slowly, 'and I shouldn't tell you anything. Meldrum must be crazy to bring you up here, unless he has some obscure plan in his mind.'

'I heard some awful noises in Greer House during the night,' she said breathlessly. 'What is it all about? Was Emily Barlow Simon Blacknall's wife?'

He nodded.

'So Adam Barlow makes groaning and banging noises during the night,' mused Melvyn Trent.

'Yes, and I wonder why Emily Barlow should marry an old madman,' returned Christine.

'I should like the answer to that, too,' said Melvyn Trent.

7

Forger's Plant

It was Melvyn Trent's opinion that little harm could befall Christine, though Stephen Meldrum's intentions were somewhat obscure. Leaving the girl a little puzzled, he wandered away with Claud Tippington.

They walked down the drive, it was true, but then Melvyn took the other's arm and guided him through the thick shrubbery. They completed a semi-circle, moving through bushes and stunted, leafy trees. Finally they emerged at the rear of the old house. They looked upon a cluster of outhouses, which were built of brick and evidently stuck on in the last few years.

Quite soon Melvyn Trent saw the man he was seeking.

'Have you fed Simon Blacknall?' asked Melvyn gently.

The other's eyes moved slowly. But he made no reply.

'Where is Simon?' asked Melvyn.

Adam Barlow's eyes suddenly fixed on his questioner's pipe. There was sudden interest in the blank blue eyes. Melvyn knew instantly there was greed, too.

Melvyn brought out a tin of tobacco and showed the little man the brown mixture. Adam Barlow stared as if fascinated. He put out a grubby hand as if to touch the tobacco. Melvyn, watching closely, gently withdrew the tin from the other's reach.

'Take me up Black Brow,' he said. 'Show me where the oil comes from. Then I'll give you this tobacco and pipe.'

Melvyn kept the pipe and tobacco tin in his hand. Adam Barlow gradually understood and with a grunt he suddenly made off along the bank of the stream.

'Not very talkative is he, Melvyn, old boy?' muttered Claud.

'This is a case where actions are of more value than words,' said Melvyn grimly.

At a plank bridge over the stream, he paused to suddenly point to a myriad-coloured swirl slowly moving down the stream.

'Oil,' he said cryptically. 'I'd like to discover how oil gets into this cool little stream.'

'Perhaps Meldrum threw some oil car waste into the stream,' suggested Claud.

'Ever heard of waterfalls providing hydraulic power?' asked the other abruptly.

He was interrupted by a hail from Claud Tippington. Claud had wandered away from the waterfall.

'I say, here's the blighter's grave. I doubt if a dead man can print slush, old boy!'

Melvyn strode across the intervening ground.

'An exhumation order would settle quite a few ideas,' he said grimly.

Adam was working his way along a ledge of the rocky glen. It seemed that he was intending to walk straight into the falling water. For a moment Melvyn was tempted to shout him back, but he reconsidered. He went after the little man instead. Claud very gingerly commenced to follow in their tracks.

When Melvyn looked up after a particularly awkward climb, he found

Adam Barlow had vanished. Because this did not make sense, he rapidly edged along the narrow catwalk to the spot. where he had last seen the little man

The waterfall was so close that his clothes were becoming damp with spray. Pausing he looked around and saw Adam standing on a ledge, which ran behind the waterfall. The little man was evidently waiting for him.

It was a tricky, damp business dashing through a thin curtain of spray and water, but soon Melvyn was beside the old man. He waited for Claud to approach.

After a decided hesitation, Claud ducked through the wet curtain and stood beside them.

'Dammit, I'm wet!' he bleated. 'And what now?'

'I think we have found what we seek,' replied Melvyn Trent.

8

The Coffin

Stephen Meldrum returned to Greer House to find two people ready with tales that confirmed his worst fears.

Emily Barlow met him first in his room.

'There is trouble brewing. Two men have been spying here — one is that fool Claud Arnell who lives in the cottage. The other must be from the police. He knew I was Simon's wife.'

'I know,' he snapped. 'They tried to intercept me when I met Manning.' He mopped his brow though the day was not very warm. 'This is the end. We must leave.'

'Nonsense. They have no evidence, though we must be very careful. We must get through the printing tonight. Everything is ready. The paper is prepared and the press is set. You are sure He will be ready?'

'Yes, yes,' he said hurriedly.

'Then we will get this latest consignment out. If we have to leave, we shall take the notes with us. But are you sure about Him?'

'I'm a doctor, aren't I?' he snarled.

She calmly assessed his panicky appearance, and her lips compressed.

'You're a doctor. That's the only reason why you stay here, and I wish you would not forget that. Incidentally, I would like you to speak to your niece. She has been talking to the man who called here a few minutes ago. Find out what she talked about.'

But Stephen Meldrum had no need to force Christine to speak. She met him in the dining room and her story burst from her.

'Uncle Stephen, I know everything! That man you brought here in your car — he is a crook! Someone at Greer House is forging money!'

'Who is the man you spoke to?'

She hesitated, and then out of pity for him gave him the truth.

'He is a special investigator employed

177

by some bank. His name is Melvyn Trent.'

He groaned, and his brown eyes were positively sick.

'We must leave,' he whispered. 'Mrs. Barlow is a dangerous woman. I think she is mad. She certainly has a dangerous greed.'

'What do you want me to do?'

'I want you to leave for London today and take a large sum of money to a certain address I will give you.'

'Is it forged money?' she choked.

He shook his head vigorously.

'Oh, no. Of course not. It is real enough money, and the address is that of a good old woman I knew — in — the — old days. She will hold the package without the slightest curiosity until I arrive. Of course, I shall have to go into hiding, but I have that all arranged.'

'But why can't you take the money with you? Oh, don't think I won't do it for you, uncle, but I don't understand.'

'I might be arrested and the money confiscated,' he muttered, and his hands actually trembled. 'It is good money, and

I need it. You will do this for me, Christine?'

'Of course. I'll go as soon as you think it necessary.'

* * *

Melvyn Trent and Claud Tippington came down Black Brow and avoided Greer House. They went to Claud's cottage and got the bicycles. They cycled into Kirkdale and called at a farm to make an unusual request. They hired two spades and paid handsomely for them.

When they were returning through Kirkdale Melvyn saw Christine making for the station, taking with her a small case.

'You are not leaving Kirkdale?' he queried when they met.

'Actually I am.' Her troubled eyes could not meet his. She wished she could confide everything in him. For in an instant she knew she hated leaving so suddenly. It was odd but she felt there were so many unsaid things they should have talked about.

'You certainly brought more luggage than you are taking away,' he joked.

'The rest will follow.'

'Has Meldrum given you this case to carry? I notice it bears his initials.'

'It — it — is his case — ' she stammered before she had time to think. Her confusion was mounting. She seized on the only excuse left to her, even though her heart sank as she gasped: 'I — I — have to catch the train. I — I — must go!'

He caught her arm.

'Why is Meldrum giving you that case? What does it contain?'

'Please!'

'But I must know,' he said sternly. 'Claud and I will go to the station with you and open the case in the waiting room. It will most likely be deserted.'

She could think of no retort or way of escape. Inside the empty waiting room, Melvyn unfastened the catches on the cheap little case. He brought out a package and tore away some of the brown paper while Claud looked reprovingly.

Under the brown paper he found wads

of new pound notes. He pulled one wad out and quickly examined them.

'Forgeries,' he said briefly, and handed them to Claud. 'I'm terribly sorry, Christine. But Stephen Meldrum can't get away with this.'

'He said the money was all genuine!' she gasped She suddenly felt utterly dismayed. Stephen had tried to trick her. He had played on her sympathy.

'What was the idea, Christine?' asked Melvyn gently. 'Is Stephen Meldrum trying to use you?'

'He — he — is leaving Greer House. He asked me to take the money to a certain address in London. I've told him about you!'

'Of course, I wanted you to do that. There is no need for you to run from Kirkdale. After this is cleared up, we've got a lot to talk about. But at the moment promise me you'll go along to Claud's cottage and stay there until we return.'

She nodded dumbly. Somehow she could not face the prospect of returning to the air of menace and mystery in Greer House.

They left her at the cottage, hiding the case of spurious money under an old floorboard. Then Melvyn and Claud continued once more up the track to the waterfall on Black Brow. They came to the grave of Simon Blacknall. It was almost completely overgrown with weeds, and would not have been easy to find had it not been for a rough wood plaque.

'What a ghastly job!' gulped Claud, and he leaned on his spade.

'Get on with it, man. We haven't time to waste.'

They soon discovered, to Claud's relief, that the coffin had not been buried at regulation depth. After three feet their spades scraped the clayey wood. After another half hour of feverish work, punctuated by curses, they cleared the coffin lid of earth. Melvyn stooped to examine the grim object.

'Very interesting,' he said. 'The lid is not screwed down.'

Claud shuddered.

Melvyn inserted the tip of his spade between the coffin and the lid and gradually levered the lid free. He bent down again and pulled the lid completely to one side.

They looked down at damp, discoloured wood, but the coffin was empty!

'Very interesting,' repeated Melvyn with satisfaction. 'It would seem that Simon Blacknall is not dead. That fixes my two irreconcilable facts.'

He stuck his spade into the earth and turned for his jacket which he had laid aside.

'Let's get down to Kirkdale. I want a warrant to search Greer House. We've got to get in touch with the police at last.'

But the words were hardly out of his mouth when an immense figure of a man lumbered through the trees towards them. His hands dangled loosely by his side. As he lumbered towards Melvyn and Claud with incredible strides, he rocked like some ill-balanced monster.

'Simon Blacknall!' breathed Melvyn Trent.

But the next instant he was fighting for his life.

9

Capitulation

The fight was very short. Melvyn Trent slogged two punches into the giant before a first struck him like a hammer head. As he fell, black unconsciousness wrapped round his brain.

He knew nothing until he stirred to life again, and then recollection was swift. Holding his throbbing head, he got to his feet and looked round for Claud Tippington.

Claud was not in sight.

Melvyn spent a few valuable minutes climbing down to the cavern under the waterfall. He armed himself with a thick branch. But the cavern was silent and deserted.

He wasted not one second. He ran up to the main entrance of Greer House and found Emily Barlow and Stephen Meldrum at the bottom of the staircase that led to the empty floors.

'You had better not stop me,' he panted. 'Simon Blacknall is alive. I think he has taken Claud Tippington to this house. If murder is done, I warn you, you are all implicated. You know what that means.'

Suddenly Stephen Meldrum shouted hoarsely:

'He has taken the young man to the closed rooms! I am not to blame! I want to confess everything. Emily sent Simon up Black Brow when he discovered you'd been up there with Adam!'

Melvyn saw the sudden movement that Emily Barlow made, and he sprang to her. Before the woman could remove the gun from the pocket in her thick black dress, he had wrenched it clear.

'You are not very quick with a revolver,' he said. 'Now quick, show me where Simon Blacknall hangs out. Quick! The game is up. There is enough evidence in the cavern under Black Brow to convict you.'

Stephen Marlowe babbled: 'I was . . . only Simon's doctor . . . kept him alive . . . when in his coma. Only kept him alive . . . I tell you! I'm not a forger. Simon is the forger . . . '

On the third floor they came to a room. The door was not locked, and he saw Claud lying motionless.

On a low couch lay an immobile figure. The giant of a man lay stretched like a corpse. Melvyn walked over to Claud and with a sigh of relief found that he was alive but unconscious. Then he stared at the white, grim features of the giant so fantastically asleep.

Stephen Meldrum's nervous words poured out the explanation: 'He is in a coma. Simon Blacknall has been in an intermittent coma for the past two years, though he is gradually throwing off the spells. It is all the result of the fall from Black Brow. When he is normal and lucid, Emily and he operate the press under Black Brow just as Simon Blacknall did before his accident. But I was simply here to tend to him during his spells of coma. That's all.'

'You're a liar!' snapped Emily Barlow. 'You snivelling coward — you accepted the profits from Simon's work.'

'I was only paid to look after Simon Blacknall!' screamed Stephen Meldrum. 'You know he nearly died in the year before I arrived. But you — you are a murderess! You killed Liz Barlow. She and Adam knew Simon was alive. They knew he wasn't in his grave! And when Liz died of ptomaine poisoning, no one suspected you! You married Adam so that he could never give evidence against you — even if anyone believed him.'

'You can quit fighting,' rapped Melvyn, as he looked up from Claud. 'The jury will decide the issue. Meldrum, carry Claud downstairs, if you have the strength.'

★   ★   ★

Christine stayed on at Kirkdale, booking a room at the Blacksmith's Arms.

'I shouldn't worry too much, Christine,' Melvyn said. 'Meldrum is definitely implicated, and if I had not brought him to book, you can be sure it was inevitable at some time or other. Still, he might get away with a lighter sentence than Emily Barlow.'

'Oh, I hope so!'

'They have both made statements,' continued Melvyn. 'This coma that attacked Simon Blacknall is very rare and occurs mostly in Eastern countries. However, if you'd like to hear the grisly details, he was definitely certified dead by a doctor. Candidly, I rather think the doctor made a somewhat perfunctory examination. But that suited Emily Barlow. Actually she arrived secretly at Greer House the day Simon Blacknall fell from Black Brow, but most of the villagers think she arrived the day he was buried. She alone realized Simon Blacknall was not actually dead. No one, except Liz and perhaps old Adam, knew she was really Simon Blacknall's wife. But Liz Barlow had sent for her. Now after the certificate of death, Simon Blacknall was buried on Black Brow. Three hours later Emily, Adam and Liz Barlow dug the earth away and brought Simon Blacknall to the empty rooms in Greer House. Perhaps another hour under the earth and he would have been really dead, for in spite of his imperceptible breathing the air in the coffin would soon become exhausted.

'Those moans and thumps you heard during the night came from Simon. Meldrum informs us he was often violent and uncontrollable, though he had lucid spells during which he directed the work in the cavern under Black Brow.'

'I hate that name,' she said vehemently. 'I shall never come back here again.'

'Oh, I don't know,' he said quietly. 'Kirkdale is a nice little place for — for — '

'For what?'

'Holidays — and — er, so on,' he finished lamely.

She flashed him a subdued smile.

'Over the hills there are some lovely lakes. I should like to see them.'

He took her arm suddenly.

'We shall see them together. I want you to — to know — Christine that — that — '

His voice trailed off, but the pressure on her hand had but one meaning.

As they disappeared down the lane, his voice could be heard still trying to explain a very simple thing.

3

THE BLOOD TRAUMA

There was no doubt that it was blood! Red, sticky and faintly sickly in odour, it formed a pool at least twelve inches wide in the luggage compartment of his car. He slowly straightened his back, assuming his normal six feet of big-boned body, while a tinge of fear crept like a poison into his bowels.

This gruesome mess was blood. The mental fixation that it was *human blood* came immediately. He remembered Betsy's wild outburst. 'I'll kill him, Dad — I'll kill him!' Her fury stuck vividly in his mind; and now blood! As for other logic — well, there were no animals in their household. No stricken dog, for instance, had made this mess . . .

Walt Beaumont slowly closed the lid of the big compartment, turning the key. Ah . . . keys . . . yes . . . Betsy had her set and she drove the car. He had been away on business all day yesterday. He had

flown two hundred miles; stayed over-
night at a small hotel. He'd done business
with old John Manton regarding the
importation of a new European car and
then returned home, arriving only half an
hour ago.

Walt changed his mind about driving
into town. He picked up the small valise
he'd been about to place in the car and
turned back to the house. He would have
to find Betsy. She should have been at
home. He really had to talk with her; try
to get some sense out of her wild young
head. She and Mick Grain had a crazy
thing going. That was all right; he didn't
mind them being young, long-haired,
unisexed and heaven knows what — until
that incredibly grim fight a week ago
when they had clawed into each other,
fists and fingernails furiously seeking to
punish, voices screaming unnaturally.

It was then that he had first suspected
drugs. He had parted them and sent Mick
packing. Betsy's hysteria had lasted an
hour and he had considered sending for
the doctor — but the nagging fear that it
was drugs deterred him. At last she had

taken a sedative and gone to bed. That night he wished his wife was still alive.

The next day he'd demanded an explanation. Betsy had been weary, like someone with a hangover, and her answers had been chaotic, evasive. Then she'd flared. 'He's a swine! You thought him clever . . . witty . . . but he's no good! I'll kill him, Dad — I'll kill him!'

She had refused to give another coherent reason for her sudden hatred of Mick Grain.

Drawing a long patient breath, he had concluded that it was all crazy talk, the sort of thing a wild girl of eighteen would fling out during a spat with her boyfriend.

Walt Beaumont went into the cool confines of the house and stood by the telephone, doubts churning his inward mental processes. Should he dial the number of the grubby house that Mick Grain shared with a pal? Or should he get down there and check for himself? Was it really human blood? How had it got into the boot?

He replaced the receiver and stared at a mirror, seeing the tight mouth and thick greying hair with critical disfavour. Yes, he was tall, straight-backed and wore good suits — but his was a generation that had spawned problem children. Betsy had always known a good home and had never been ignored. She had just gone wild, that was all. And now he had to do something about it. He had, for one thing, to discover why a pool of blood was in the boot of his car. And he had to find Betsy.

Changing his mind once again, with understandable doubts assailing him, he went back to the car, climbed in and started the engine. Within ten minutes he had driven through the city streets and was parked almost opposite the third-class shops that sandwiched the old house between them. He knew the spot. Betsy had got him to drive her down more than once when she was visiting Mick Grain. He had never been inside the flat. He'd been told the young man shared it with a friend.

'Mick prefers to live his life his way,' Betsy had said. 'His mother put him out of her home.'

'What does he work at?'

'He's still a student.' Her clear blue eyes had defied him to make critical comment.

Walt Beaumont looked at some cards in the main entrance to the building. In a rack of six he spotted the two names bracketed together: Mick Grain/Hec Dalton. Second floor.

He climbed stairs that creaked under a thin carpet. The second flight creaked and were bare, scuffed wood. He came to a landing and searched the doors. He saw the card with the double names again. He knocked.

Waiting, he hoped to see the door open and Mick, with his clean-cut face, beaky nose and long hair, stand inquiringly before him. That would settle one impossible suspicion. But there was no reply to his second and third knock. He tried the door handle and it opened with an ease that seemed oddly taunting.

A small lobby and then a room; and this was so madly untidy that it rocked him — and then he realized with a shock that a broken chair, a shattered vase, books that had obviously been hurled around and a shattered table lamp were not the norm even for the craziest of students. Someone had been fighting in here!

He walked around, avoiding a dollop of food on the worn carpet. He halted and bent down to examine the broken plate and congealed food. After a few moments he decided the mess of eggs, bacon and beans had been on the floor for some time — hours, possibly a day. The stuff was horribly gluey, reminding him of the other gruesome patch in his car.

He had never considered himself a wildly imaginative man, but there were certain flights of fancy, which, he shrewdly realized, were conditioned into his mind by works of fiction, television plays and movies. He was a city man, channeled to think according to modern TV culture, and a fight in a room and blood in his car linked crazy mental images.

Betsy had had the keys to the car! Where was she now? More important, where was Mick Grain? Could she and

Mick have done this damage during a fight? Had there been another fight between the two of them while he was away?

Walking grimly around the room, it struck him that there was another tenant in this apartment — Mick's pal, Hec Dalton. Where was he? Surely he knew about this damage and — hope rising in his reasoning mind — maybe he and Mick Grain had been fighting?

With a curt laugh at his own imperfections, Walt Beaumont realized his imagination was permeated with every trick in the mass entertainment world. His mind seethed with three turbulent thoughts . . . the awful pool of blood . . . this damaged room . . . and Betsy's screaming threat . . . 'I'll kill him!'

He took out his cigarettes; lit one and inhaled. He was, he thought, being fooled by these vivid factors. There could — and would — be reasonable explanations for the blood and the smashed furniture, and Betsy's threat was merely one of hysteria!

He suddenly knew he was being watched and he whipped around. A tall, calm-faced girl stood in the doorway, her half-smile and long dark hair almost Mona Lisa in effect.

'Who are you?' He gestured with the cigarette.

'I'm Toni Bruce. And you?'

'Betsy Beaumont's father . . . why are you here . . . do you know Mick Grain?'

'Yes — and Hec. Real groovy men . . . '

He pointed swiftly at the room. 'How did this happen?'

'There was a fight . . . '

'I can see that!' He directed his anger at her. 'Who fought?'

She walked into the room, her flared slacks tight against her long thighs, her weird floral jacket flapping against bra-less contours. She was almost as tall as he. Her calm and grace fed his antagonism. 'Ah . . . who fought?' she murmured. 'You won't dig this, Daddy — because it was our dreamy Mick and your cat of a daughter.'

'Betsy and Mick Grain fought here? When?'

'Yesterday. They lost their cool — not for the first time — and threw the bric-a-brac around . . . '

'Do you know where I can find Betsy?' he asked savagely. 'She isn't at home . . . '

'Perhaps she has taken off! It's a big world . . . '

'Taken off? Where to?'

'How should I know?' The coolness faded. 'Get out of here! I want to straighten up.'

'I'll wait for Betsy to return home,' he snapped. 'But maybe you can tell me where to find Mick . . . '

She interrupted him with a sudden spasm of fury that astounded him because the transition was so swift. Her arm swung; almost grabbed at a bronze ashtray but halted at the last moment. 'Go easy, damn you! You don't belong here!'

'Maybe if I could find this Hec Dalton I'd get more help out of him,' he challenged.

'Ha! That's a laugh! You don't know how funny that is! Hec! He doesn't help anybody. He makes on people! Yeah — we're all profit to the beautiful Hec!'

'Tell me where he is!'

'Get out of my hair!' She moved

201

around and tried to pick up the pieces of broken vase. Her hands trembled, he noticed. Gone was the façade of insolent, youthful calm. 'You don't want Hec. Go talk to Betsy — the bitch!'

'You hate her,' he stated.

'I think I hate everybody . . . '

Walt Beaumont went to the door, pausing grimly. 'You sicken me! You're unbalanced! Is it just hate — or drugs — or too much money — or too much time? You've got everything — youth — chances — and yet nothing.' He pointed a stern finger. 'But forget my generalizations: product of my age group. I know one thing; you're trying to trick me.'

'Do you really think so?' she sneered.

He gripped the door handle. 'I'll find out the truth without you — Mick — Betsy — this Hec — '

The process of walking to his car was automatic. He set down and gripped the wheel until his knuckles showed white.

He took the car on course through crowded streets. Parked vehicles, traffic lights, pedestrians — they were all navigated with perfect control, and then he was home, the car stationary before his garage. He sat still.

So Mick and Betsy had fought in the flat according to Toni Bruce — but a fight was a long way from a killing. On the other hand a pool of blood in a car boot was always a sign of some grisly crime. He'd read about it, in newspapers where facts were reported and not fancies. A big car boot could carry a body.

Walt Beaumont slid out of the driving seat. He was a fool to link these bizarre situations, which happened only to other people, with Betsy and her adolescent rages. He'd go indoors and have a stiff drink.

He was holding the glass when the telephone demanded his attention. He went over. 'Yes?'

'Oh, Dad — you're back . . . '

'Where are you, Betsy? I want to talk to you. I want you to come home.'

'This electronic wand enables us to talk . . . '

'I want to show you something. Now come over here right away!'

'I can't — I'm busy . . . '

'Where the devil are you? What're you doing?' he shouted. The phone pressed hard against his ear.

'Why are you so angry?'

'Look here — did you use my car yesterday while I was away?'

'Er — yes — I did . . . why lose your cool? I didn't bump anything . . . '

'Have you been fighting with Mick Grain again?'

'We always fight,' came the cool response.

'Don't be evasive! Have you — you — attacked him — like you did a week ago?'

'I want to forget that . . . '

He almost screamed back; his nerves were taut. 'Don't try to be smart! Did you fight in his apartment?'

'No.'

'Now, look, my girl . . . ' His voice was thick with controlled impatience. 'Come back to the house — now! I want to show you something. Just drop whatever you're doing. I want you home to show you something and don't be so damned defiant!'

'Oh, boy — heavy stuff. Just what is it, dear father?'

'A pool of blood in my car!' he yelled stridently and slammed the phone down before he realized how melodramatic was the action and the fact that he didn't know where she was and couldn't ring back.

He went back to the living room and sat down, staring sombrely at nothing. There were only two real facts; blood in his car boot and the smashed-up apartment. Betsy's threats could be dismissed as hysteria . . . surely . . . a feasible assumption . . .

And yet his recollection of that fight in his own home, when they'd torn into each other like two young animals, flushed away his attempt to rationalise everything. In that momentary madness they had hated each other. Could young people hate like this while they professed love? She had said later that he was no good — a swine and other epithets. Of course sex attraction in the young could be a love/hate relationship, a battle of the sexes. Half-an-hour's reading of the right text books could establish that. He had always wanted Betsy to enjoy the very zest of being young, sure that she would weather her stormy adolescence. Now why had she described Mick Grain as no good and a swine? Certainly from the standards of an older man he was a bit of a lunatic. Was there something else?

Walt Beaumont stared wearily around the room, seeing the furnishings as mere familiar things. There were no details in the clock, the pictures, the glassware cabinet. The TV stood like a box, the now silent dispenser of preconceived ideas. He felt hungry but unable to consider searching for food. He thought he should telephone the police about the pool of blood. They could establish that it was human or otherwise, and also group it. Perhaps he should clean up the mess and remain silent; that would depend on Betsy. Where the devil was she? Now if Margot was still alive they would have been able to talk this over . . . find some solace in each other's opinions . . . she knew how to handle Betsy. Looking back, it seemed that the girl had got wilder since her mother's death.

Walt Beaumont stirred and got to his feet; Margot was dead; he was alone. He'd have to handle it his way, realizing that these facts were not a TV situation.

The sound of her footsteps whirled him around to face her. She searched his eyes, her clear-skinned prettiness a reminder of Margot. 'Father, dear father — what's with your car? Are you trying to annoy me . . . get me back to the parental nest? A pool of blood, you said?' She was mocking, her long, corn-coloured hair wisping across her face. She was wearing her blue trouser suit, the lightweight material clinging to firm curves.

In spite of his anxiety, his annoyance returned. He immediately flared back: 'I said blood and I mean that! In the luggage compartment of the car! Do you know anything about it?'

'No.' She laughed. 'Sure you didn't cut your finger, Daddy, dear?'

'A pool of blood! More than a pint, I'd say: I'll show you it — a horrible gory mess. You — you — know nothing about it?'

'Why should I?'

'You haven't fought with Mick Grain? I mean — attacked him — the way you two went for each other a week ago — almost trying to kill each other!'

'That's all over. I told you I want to forget about it . . . '

'You were on some damned drug!' He glared, pointing a finger.

'Okay — we were experimenting. We were fools! But it's over . . . '

Walt patted his pockets for his pack of cigarettes; found them and worried the carton. 'Over, is it? And you haven't had a violent fight at his flat — mashing the place up?'

She stared without amusement. 'No.'

Exasperated, he threw it at her. 'I've just been over to that place, hoping to find Mick, and everything is broken up. There *has* been a fight — and I met a girl called Toni Bruce. She said you and Mick had a violent fight — or her contemporary words to that effect.'

Betsy began to laugh and walked gracefully around the room. 'Oh, dear — Toni is such a liar! She hates me! Correction — we dislike each other. It's glandular — or something — and of course Mick and Hec haven't helped by throwing us together . . . '

'Will you take this seriously?' he shouted. 'There's a pool of blood in my car and that apartment has been smashed up. Can you explain that? Has something happened to Mick? That's what I want to know . . . '

For some moments Betsy Beaumont became a perturbed young woman and she slowly found words. 'Really — Dad — did you think that? You — thought — I attacked Mick — and blood in the car — you really fell for that gimmicky 'body in the boot' situation. Is that the way of it, Dad?'

'It damned well is!' he ground out. 'You threatened to kill him — remember?'

She laughed uncertainly. 'That's crazy! Did I say that?'

'You also said he was a swine and no good . . . '

'Oh, Dad — how can I say it — that was just fool talk! I love him, Dad! Really, truly, love him! He's a beautiful man! Of course, he's good! You shouldn't take any notice of me . . . '

Walt Beaumont whipped around in anger. 'Answer me one thing — where is Mick Grain now?'

'Right here, Mr. Beaumont.'

The clear male voice held no jocularity as the living room door swished close to the broadloom carpet. Mick Grain stood there, tall, long-legged, floral shirt, hair hanging loosely to his shoulders. His face was set; his lips tight.

'I've just been sorting things out in the back of an old car I've just bought,' he said. 'I brought Betsy along. She's been helping me arrange a new flat over in Stilmore Avenue.'

Walt stared. 'You're all right? You're not hurt? I mean . . . '

'I know what you mean, Mr. Beaumont and it's about time someone tried to explain. I overheard Betsy talking about a body in the luggage compartment . . . '

'There's blood — a lot of it — in the car.'

'I know. There has been a body in that compartment . . . '

Betsy repeated like any woman. Her

hand shot to her mouth. Walt Beaumont waited grimly.

'I asked Betsy for the loan of your car yesterday,' said Mick Grain quietly. 'That's how the blood got there. But let me say something else first: Betsy and I might be young and foolish, but we love each other. Yes, we did try drugs — Hec peddled them! We're finished with that — two trips were enough! I don't want to tear at Betsy physically — and she doesn't want to hurt me. She thought me a swine when Toni Bruce told her we'd made love — but that I can swear to you was another example of Toni's facility for stinking lies. Betsy won't be seeing Toni again — and I won't be seeing Hec. As I say, I've got another place to live — and I have to study. And I won't be using your car — I've got an old heap.'

Walt Beaumont walked uncertainly; gripped the young man's arm. 'Tell me — the blood — you said there had been a body — '

'Yes — Hec Dalton.'

'He's dead?'

'No. Oh, Toni thought he was dead

— after she had fought with him at our place and knocked him unconscious with a bronze ornament. She hit him on the head — she's pretty quick at reaching for things to throw. They were both high, I think. I arrived in the middle of the party — about two minutes after she had clobbered him. He looked dead and I — I — panicked, too. She pleaded with me to help her. I rushed over to see Betsy . . . I didn't explain anything . . . just said could I have a loan of the car. When I got back to the apartment, Hec was still lying like a corpse. I suppose I'm a bit nervy at times — panic was still there — Toni was insisting I take him away — just dump the body — '

'You got him into the car locker? How? I mean, didn't anyone see you coming down the stairs to the street?'

'There's a back entrance, a flight of old stairs hardly ever used. I'd parked the car at the back — so we bundled Hec into the luggage locker . . . He was bleeding!'

'A fool thing to do!' Walt Beaumont exploded.

'I agree. I had hardly got a few streets

away when I sort of recovered my cool. I drove to the hospital. Hec is there now, suffering from some sort of concussion. Toni will lie her way through it all, I suppose . . . '

Betsy swung. 'Oh, Mick, why didn't you tell me?'

'I was getting around to it . . . it isn't pretty . . . I'd have told you!'

Walt went to the sideboard and picked up a bottle of whisky with a slightly unsteady hand. 'Thank God that's all it is! I never realized I had such fool fixations — but never mind. There's one thing you should have done, Mick.'

'What's that?'

'You should have cleaned out that compartment! It would have saved me an awful lot of trauma!'

THE END

We do hope that you have enjoyed reading this large print book.

Did you know that all of our titles are available for purchase?

We publish a wide range of high quality large print books including:
Romances, Mysteries, Classics
General Fiction
Non Fiction and Westerns

Special interest titles available in large print are:
The Little Oxford Dictionary
Music Book, Song Book
Hymn Book, Service Book

Also available from us courtesy of Oxford University Press:
Young Readers' Dictionary
(large print edition)
Young Readers' Thesaurus
(large print edition)

For further information or a free brochure, please contact us at:
Ulverscroft Large Print Books Ltd.,
The Green, Bradgate Road, Anstey,
Leicester, LE7 7FU, England.
Tel: (00 44) **0116 236 4325**
Fax: (00 44) **0116 234 0205**

Other titles in the
Linford Mystery Library:

MURDER, MYSTERY AND MAGIC

John Burke

An innocent man is arrested for a murder committed by a woman . . . A guilty man confesses to another murder — but the police arrest an innocent woman! A man finds the woman of his dreams — and finds he's in a nightmare . . . The tenants of a new block of flats are so delighted with their new home that they don't really want to go out — little realizing that they *can't* leave. Strange incidents from macabre stories of *Murder, Mystery . . . and Magic.*

THE WAGER

E. C. Tubb

Captain Tom Mason of Homicide has a peculiarly horrible case to deal with. He investigates a murder where the victim has been decapitated. However, only the body remains at the crime scene. The murderer appears to have taken the head as a grisly trophy. Prompt police action, as they cordon off the area, yields four suspects. One of them, identified as running from the scene, is held in custody — but then another three people are decapitated . . .

THE WHITE FRIAR

Donald Stuart

Alexander Kielmann pursued his nefarious activities with impunity . . . blackmail, burglary, even murder. At Scotland Yard there were suspicions, but no proof available. Then Kielmann received a letter: *'You have ruined lives, but death is waiting for you . . . Your associates will suffer . . . They will receive their just deserts, you yourself being reserved for the last. I am Death, and I enclose my card.'* A visiting card showed a drawing of a monk in a white habit and cowl. Who was the *White Friar*?

CURTAIN CALL

Geraldine Ryan

It seemed too good an opportunity to miss . . . Impoverished by her father's death, Kate Spenser has been forced to give up music lessons, despite her talent. So when the enigmatic pianist John Hawksley comes to stay with her wealthy neighbours, Kate cannot resist asking him to teach her. She was not to know Hawksley's abrupt manner would cause friction between them, nor that the manipulative Euphemia would set out to ensnare the one man who seemed resistant to her charms . . .